# Wagering HOME

## C. M. BOERS

ISBN-10: 0-9906452-9-0
ISBN-13: 978-0-9906452-9-0

# DEDICATION

Like many things in life, this book took me on a different path than I
ever thought it would. But that is the way life goes and because of that,
I'd like to dedicate this book to my Mom. She's always been the one who
stood with me and continues to do so whenever I need her to no matter
what life throws at us. Thanks Mom.

# Chapter ONE

**BEEP. BEEP. BEEP.**

"Has there been any change?" A woman's voice broke through the darkness.

"No, she . . ." The muffled reply faded away.

It's quiet. Nothing tugged at me like the place of constant beeping.

Every now and then, the beeping place pulled me back. The noise there hurt my head, but even here the dull ache never completely left.

***

*Beep. Beep. Beep.*

*Not here again. Please.*

"We're doing everything we can, ma'am. She's breathing on her own, and brain activity is good. We have to give her time to heal."

A woman sobbed.

*Ow. Please stop. That hurts.*

"Doctor, how long do you think it'll be?" a man asked.

"There's really no way to tell. She'll wake when she's ready."

The voices drifted away again in a fog. Silence once again filled my head.

*Thank you.*

***

*Beep. Beep.*

Aside from the beeping, the room was still. The ache in my head seemed to be diminishing. Voices from farther away floated toward me. And ringing. A phone, maybe?

I groaned.

"Melanie?" a woman's voice said from beside me. "Melanie? Can you hear me?"

*Who's Melanie?*

"I'll go get the nurse," a man said with urgency, his voice fading, along with his footsteps.

I couldn't move anything. At first. I kept trying, thinking only of my hand. Then slowly, my finger twitched.

I moaned. Behind my eyelids, it wasn't dark anymore. My left foot slid against the sheet, the other remained stuck in place.

"Did I hear that right? She's waking up?" a different woman, older maybe, said.

"She moved and made some noises." The first woman's voice contained an edge of hope.

"Melanie, my name is Wendy. I'm a nurse here at the hospital. Can you hear me?" the older woman said.

*Melanie? Is she talking to me? Is that my name?*

I couldn't will myself to speak. The words wouldn't come.

*Beep. Beep. Beep.*

"Melanie, I'm going to hold your left hand. Can you squeeze it for me?"

Something closed around my hand, and I moved my finger under its weight.

"'Atta girl." The older woman chuckled.

A strangled sob came from the other side of me.

"Melanie, can you open your eyes for me now?"

*Eyes?* I whimpered. *That lets the light in, doesn't it?*

I pulled my hand, but something tugged against my elbow. I reached with my other hand to unharness my arm, only to be stopped.

"Don't mess with those IVs, sweetheart," Wendy said.

My eyes fluttered open. Though they didn't clear right away, whiteness faded, giving way to shapes. Then, all at once, faces came into focus. Three of them stared at me. Waiting. Hopeful.

"Well, hello there, Melanie. It's nice to see your beautiful blue eyes. Can you say something?" The nurse, Wendy, crossed her arms, watching me.

"W-" I croaked.

"Here, try some water."

Tears poured down the other woman's face, the one who didn't wear scrubs.

*Why is she crying? Why am I here?*

"Who is . . ." I thought hard about what they kept calling me. "Melanie?"

The sobbing woman opened her mouth to speak but froze, looking at the others in the room. I focused on the nurse.

The nurse just eyed me, expectant.

*Why won't anyone answer me?*

"What's your name?" the nurse finally asked.

My name? I hadn't even thought about it. It didn't come to me. And when I didn't answer, the nurse's face changed to concern.

"What's your name, sugar?" she asked again.

"I-I don't know."

What did that mean? Was my name really Melanie? Who forgot their own name?

"Something's wrong . . ." I bit my lip.

"It's okay," the nurse said.

It didn't feel okay.

"Do you remember anything?" the sobbing woman asked.

I rubbed my hand on the rough blanket. Something nagged at the back of my thoughts. It told me I should know who she was, yet nothing about her seemed familiar. I felt no closer to her than I did the window filled with cards or vases of flowers that filled the table below them. But she sat near me, crying at my bedside. That meant something. One didn't cry at a stranger's hospital bed.

"I'm sorry," I whispered.

The woman buried her face in the man's chest. His face creased with worry as though he held back all the emotion the woman couldn't.

"Maybe it would be a good time to take a walk." Wendy rubbed her shoulder.

The man nodded and ushered the woman from the room.

"Do you remember anything about them?" She pulled a tablet against her body.

I searched my thoughts for anything, but nothing came. A knot settled in the pit of my stomach. I looked down at my feet protruding from the blanket, one appearing bigger than the other.

"I see. Don't worry. Give yourself time. You'll remember." She bent down and whispered, "They're your parents."

***

"Well, look at you." A girl who looked no older than eighteen wheeled herself into the room. "You're finally awake."

I rubbed the sudden pain shooting in my temple. "Uh, do I know you?"

An exaggerated look of shock crossed her face, and she grasped her chest. "I'm hurt you don't remember me—your very best friend."

"I'm sorry . . . I—"

She laughed. "I'm just kidding." Then her tanned face scrunched. "We've never officially met. I'm Grace." She pointed at her legs. "Spine injury. I fell off my horse like a dummy."

"I'm sorry."

"Is that all you ever are? Sorry?" She made to put her hand on her hip, but the wheelchair got in the way. "Do you have a name?"

I didn't answer.

"Hello?"

"I can't remember, but they're calling me Melanie." I picked at the blanket hem.

She wheeled her way to the end of the bed and grabbed the tablet the nurse had left behind.

"Yep. That's what it says. Melanie."

I shrugged.

"You really don't remember anything?"

I shook my head. I didn't know how I should feel about her getting to see that when I hadn't.

"No wonder you were so apologetic for not knowing me." She chuckled and continued thumbing through my chart. "Broken leg. Collapsed lung. Broken ribs. Dislocated collarbone. Concussion. Multiple lacerations." She blew out a breath. "You're a mess."

She took stock of my injuries like she was reading a grocery list, and I could distinctly feel each one. "I feel like a mess."

"Well, you were out long enough."

"I almost wish I still was. It's like I've woken up to a nightmare."

"Eh, it could be worse."

I lifted my head to look at her. She must be insane. "How?"

"Psh." She waved me off. "So, those your folks?"

I stared at her.

"The ones Wendy shooed out of here," she added.

"Oh." I bit my cheek. "I guess."

"Right . . . you don't remember. My folks don't come in much anymore. Can't take any more time off work, ya know?"

I remained quiet as the ache in my head, and everywhere else, intensified.

Nurse Wendy strolled back into the room, took one look at Grace, and grinned.

"Couldn't wait a moment longer, could you?"

Grace smirked. "Of course not. She's the only one here even close to my age."

"Shouldn't you be at physical therapy?" She rested her arms across her chest.

Grace didn't answer but looked at me sheepishly.

"Go on, get out of here. Give Melanie time to rest."

"Oh, fine. I'll be back though." She winked at me and wheeled herself out.

Wendy handed me a small cup. "Those should help with the pain."

They felt like glass going down my throat, and I grabbed the foam cup from the tray beside me, gulping water to soothe the ache.

"Now, just sit back and relax. Lunch will be here in a few minutes."

My stomach grumbled just thinking about it. "Can you tell me how long it's been?"

Wendy looked at the clipboard in her hands. She rubbed her forehead as if debating whether to answer.

"It's not important," she said.

"It is to me," I whispered, though not on purpose.

"Two days."

I'd missed two days in what felt like no time at all. I nodded, feeling as though I owed her that much for her honesty.

Nurse Wendy left the room with muted steps, and I sank into sleep again until the sound of sniffles interrupted the darkness.

*Beep. Beep. Beep.*

My eyes fluttered open. Someone had dimmed the lights while I slept. I rolled my head toward the sniffles and saw the woman from earlier sitting alone, blotting her eyes with a tissue. I watched her, noticing the precise movement of her hand as it brushed the tissue along her face. Her shoulder-length blonde hair hung loosely on the sides of her face, partially shielding her eyes from my gaze. Curiosity filled me with questions about her.

She looked up, putting a halt to my thoughts. Her tear-filled eyes met mine, and I didn't know what to say to her. I'd caused her pain.

"Hi, baby."

"H—" I couldn't push words from my tight throat. I swallowed against the dryness, but it was useless. I had no words to say to her anyway. I cleared my throat and offered her an apologetic smile.

She sat up straight, grabbed the cup from my table, and held the straw to my lips. It seemed a bit too close for my comfort, but her eyes lit up at the opportunity to help, so I drank.

I leaned back against the bed, allowing her to put the water back on the table. "Hi."

She smiled.

"I'm sorry," I said.

"For what, baby?"

What, exactly, was I sorry for? That I didn't remember her? That I was lying in a hospital bed in the first place? That I'd made a choice, whatever that may have been, that brought us both to this point?

"For all of this, I guess."

"You didn't cause this." Her hands remained folded in her lap.

I didn't know what else to say, so I rolled onto my back and looked at the ceiling.

"Dad went home," she offered. "He should be back soon."

I nodded.

"He's going to bring some pictures from home, and a few things from your room." She paused, as if hoping I'd say something. "We thought, maybe, it might make you feel more at home."

"Thanks."

Awkward silence followed. She continued to watch out the window. For a while, I lay there, somewhere between consciousness yet fully aware of the weight of everything I faced.

My mother cleared her throat beside me. "I know you don't remember me, but we know you. I want you to know we'll be here with you every step of the way, as much as we can be. I don't want you to think about anything other than getting better. Okay?"

I turned back to face her. "Okay."

"Good. No more saying you're sorry or feeling bad . . . for anything."

I smiled but instantly regretted it when pain sliced through my cheek. My fingers brushed the tender skin.

"Is there a mirror I can use?" I asked.

"Oh, umm, let me check the bathroom." She disappeared for a moment and returned with a small hand-held mirror.

I took a deep breath before I held it up, nervous about what I might find. A fading black eye, lined with a small cut on my cheekbone on the right side, and a yellowing bruise on my forehead on the left. Beneath it all, I was beautiful. My bright blue eyes shone through it all, standing out the most. I studied myself for probably longer than normal.

"There he is," Mom said.

The same man from before, Dad, walked in carrying a box. I put the mirror down and watched him enter. He set the box on the counter by the sink and made his way over to me.

"How's my little girl doing?" he asked, looking right into my eyes. His hand found mine, and he gave it a small squeeze.

"I don't know yet."

He smiled. "We'll figure it out."

Mom started to unload the box, setting picture frames nearest to me. Pictures of me with my parents, as well as pictures with other people I didn't recognize.

I squinted, trying to see them more clearly. Dad grabbed the one I'd been trying the hardest to see. It was me, and after he handed it to me, I could see it clearly—a boy stood next to me.

Dad watched me inspect it. He waited. But when I still said nothing, he sat on the edge of the bed. "Does he look familiar?"

"Ted! We aren't supposed to ask."

I glanced up at her. "What? What aren't you supposed to ask?"

Mom nervously fidgeted with her hands. She didn't want to answer.

"The doctor said if we push you too much or ask you too many questions, it could prevent you from remembering . . ."

"I don't think he meant what I asked," Dad said.

"It's fine." I looked at the photo again. "No, he doesn't. Who is it?"

"That's Jeremy," Dad said.

I glanced at him again, with his arm around me, my face pressed against his shoulder. My hand rested on the boy's chest. *Jeremy's* chest.

"Is he my . . . boyfriend?" I asked.

Mom nodded. "Almost a year now, I think."

If we were together for so long, why isn't he here? Unless . . .

"He was in the car, wasn't he?" I asked, yet I already knew the answer.

Mom's lips went tight before she nodded.

I peered into her eyes, searching for something that could tell me he was okay. Without any knowledge of him, I still worried harm had come to him. Somewhere deep inside of me, I must care for him, even though I had no recollection of him.

"He's okay," Mom said. "They released him yesterday."

I handed the frame back to Dad.

"What happened?" I asked. "The crash, I mean."

"A car ran a red light. They hit the passenger side . . . where you were."

"That's why I'm so messed up."

Dad nodded. "The police think the other driver fell asleep at the wheel."

I breathed in deep. Three families affected by some tragic accident.

"Are the others okay?" I asked.

"The police wouldn't say."

After Mom finished unpacking the box, she handed me two books and a single envelope.

I slid my finger under the flap and pulled out the card. My eyes watered and stung as tears pressed their way out.

It was a get well soon card signed by so many people. So many. Yet I didn't recognize a single name.

"Oh honey, what's wrong?" Mom asked.

"I don't know who any of these people are." I sobbed.

"This was too much. I'm sorry. Here, I'll put it on the table."

I handed it over with the books. I didn't know what their pages held, but I couldn't bear to look at them. Not now.

I wiped away the tears and turned away from all the pictures staring back at me from the table by the window. However well-meaning, having all of it there made me feel so much worse.

My parents whispered to each other in the corner. Didn't they already know how much of an outsider I felt? Their whispers twisted in my gut.

"Honey, we're going to go to give you some time to rest," Dad said.

"We don't have to if you want us to stay . . ." Mom said, letting it hang there, waiting for me to tell her to stay.

"No. It's okay."

She kissed me on the forehead and walked to the door. Dad squeezed my hand on his way out, and they were gone. I didn't expect to feel so much relief as I watched them walk away.

# Chapter TWO

**SUNLIGHT FILTERED THROUGH** the crack in the curtains. Just enough to cast a thin beam on the floor.

I blinked a few times, pushing the sleep from my eyes. Sleeping was rough. Every time I moved, it hurt or monitors pulled at me. The nurse checked on me throughout the night, waking me each time I'd managed to drift off.

A breakfast tray sat on the rolling table pushed up against the bed, just within reach. I lifted the lid, almost afraid of what I might find—hospital food wasn't exactly crave-able. Oatmeal and fruit. Could be worse.

I'd just taken the first bite when a soft knock sounded on the door. I swallowed the thick lump of oatmeal and turned to the door, grateful for a distraction from the not-so-great breakfast.

Jeremy stood in the doorway. I recognized him right away from the picture sitting next to me. His sandy blond hair hung to his blue eyes. He looked the same, except for a black eye and cut on his lip. His right arm was held in a sling.

"Can I come in?" he asked.

"Sure."

He stepped inside and sat on the edge of the chair next to the bed.

"How are you feeling?"

"It hurts . . ." I said. "Everywhere."

He nodded and looked to the floor. "Your parents didn't want me to come."

"Why?"

"They were worried it might upset you. They said . . . you don't remember . . ." There was a sadness in his voice as he let the words fall away, his eyes searching mine.

I pulled my lips between my teeth, unsure of how to tell him I didn't remember a single thing. I settled for shaking my head.

"I'm really sorry. I should have seen them coming . . . I should have done something. If I had—"

"This isn't something you expect. There's no way you could have prevented it."

He was silent for a while. I looked at my breakfast and took a bite. "Do you mind if I call the nurse? I could really use some pain medicine."

"Let me." He jumped up and disappeared into the hall.

There was no need to go out there, with the button to call her right there, but I imagined, being in his shoes, I would want to do anything I could to help.

I pushed my breakfast around my plate, nibbling here and there as I did, waiting for his return.

Wendy appeared, with Jeremy at her heels. She poured water from my pitcher into a foam cup and handed the pills to me.

"How are we feeling today?"

"Better than yesterday."

"That's good news. Maybe we can get you up on crutches today."

My eyebrows rose. "Uh . . . maybe."

She chuckled. "The sooner you get up, the sooner you can leave."

"Well, if that's all I've got to do to bust out of here, then sign me up."

"You got it. I'll come back in a bit to check vitals after you finish eating."

"Thanks."

She left the room, and I turned back to Jeremy, who'd settled himself back in the chair. He looked unsure, nervous somehow.

I started eating.

Jeremy didn't seem to know what to say. And it wasn't like I did. He was like a complete stranger, yet the way he looked at me, I could see his affection for me. How did one begin to put the pieces of their life back together if they didn't even know what the puzzle looked like? How could I even begin?

"Where were we going?"

"Huh?" Jeremy's eyes met mine.

"Where were we going when we got into the accident?"

A half-grin pushed up his cheek, exposing a dimple. "We'd just left dinner. We decided to go to our place. The preserve. You wanted to skip rocks at the pond in the moonlight. You wanted to see the ripples in the reflection of the moon. The moon was really bright that night, beautiful."

"That sounds nice."

"Yeah, it would have been." Regret hung on his words.

"You said, 'our place' . . ."

"Yeah. Almost a year ago, we went walking the trails there. Along the way, you pulled me to the side, and under the shade of some enormous trees right by the pond . . . you told me you loved me."

I smiled hearing him speak about our place—I only wished I remembered it.

No longer hungry, I pushed the rolling table aside.

"You okay?"

I nodded.

"No, you aren't." He stood. "I've upset you."

I looked up at him, unsure of what to say to make it better. Nothing came. I swallowed hard.

He grabbed a piece of paper from the counter and wrote down something. He picked it up and made his way back over to the bed, stopping next to me.

"Your cell was destroyed in the accident. This is my number. Call me anytime. And if you want me here, I'll be here in minutes, no matter what time. I promise. I'm here for you, no matter what." Jeremy bent, pressing his hand to the crown of my head. He rested his lips on my forehead and inhaled deep, then turned and walked out.

I ached for him to come back, but not for me; for him. Somehow, it seemed as if leaving wasn't what he wanted, yet I made no move to stop him.

After a while, sitting in silence, I flipped on the TV, but I soon found I disliked it. Maybe I always did. I couldn't know for sure.

I shut it off and settled my hands in my lap. This was going to be a long day. What did I normally do to occupy myself?

It seemed suddenly urgent that I knew—*Who am I?*

I eyed the table where my parents had stowed the picture frames and books they'd brought.

I glanced down at my broken leg and back at the table. I debated calling the nurse, but I hated to bother her just to get me something. Instead, I threw off the blanket and lifted my casted leg off the bed, draping my other next to it.

Inching my butt to the edge was a painstakingly slow process. I pressed off the bed railings and immediately regretted it when pain ripped through my ribcage. I took deep breaths, trying to breathe through it. Then my bare foot hit the cold tile, and it was like I'd finally begun living again.

On one foot, I brought myself upright, keeping my broken leg off the ground. At first I thought I could use the rolling table as a crutch, until it rolled away from me each time I hopped, making my ribs burn. I shoved it away and smiled to myself when hopping unassisted didn't hurt as bad. It was a small victory when I made it to the table, but when I stacked the books on top of each other, I realized maybe this had been shortsighted. Hopping back with the heavy books in my arms wouldn't be easy. I heaved them up, cradling them on one side.

The first hop was fine, but the second sent everything wobbling, including me. My free arm flailed, trying to balance. As a last-ditch effort, I lunged, tossing the books to the bed as I crashed to the floor, taking the water pitcher on the table down with me.

Ice cold water splashed everywhere. I sucked in as it made contact with my skin.

"Ow!" I cried out as my butt hit the floor, the impact vibrating through my spine. Tears stung my eyes.

A nurse appeared in the doorway within seconds. "What happened?"

She bent quickly, trying to get the table moved, then turned her attention back to me.

"I was trying to get those books." I pointed to the books sprawled across the bed.

"You should have called for help. You don't even have crutches yet." She picked up the pitcher and mopped up the water with the towels by the sink. "Are you hurt?"

"Besides my ego . . . and a sore butt, not any more than before." I pulled at the fabric of the wet hospital gown clinging to my legs.

"Good. Let's get you up." She leaned over and hoisted me up by my armpits. My hospital gown flapped open, revealing my backside. The nurse quickly shut it as she slid her hand down my side, helping support me in every way she could as I hopped back to the bed. I dropped onto the mattress and scooted back into place, but she didn't cover me up.

She walked over to the drawers next to the sink and pulled out a long nightgown.

"Your parents brought you some pajamas so you'd be more comfortable. Would you like to put some on?"

"Yes, please." Getting out of this stiff, bleach-smelling, wet hospital gown sounded amazing.

"Okay, I'll get you a warm washcloth to freshen up, too. Lean forward, and I'll untie you."

She undid my hospital gown and stepped back. "Can you manage on your own, or would you like me to help?"

"No, I've got it." It was bad enough she'd already seen my behind.

She nodded, then headed into the bathroom, returning with a washcloth and dry towel. "Wendy will be in to check on you in a bit."

She closed the door behind herself, and I threw the stiff hospital gown to the floor, then proceeded to clean myself up. I couldn't wait to take a real shower. I felt so much better, even after the miniscule sponge bath, as I slid the soft nightgown over my head.

Across the room, I spotted a hamper. I lifted the washcloth above my head and tossed it with a flick of my wrist. The door swung open again, and Grace pushed herself into the room. The towel fell to the floor right in front of her. Her eyebrows raised.

My cheeks heated. "I missed."

"I see that. They don't have you up yet?"

"We will right now," Wendy said as she rounded the corner. "Sounds like you tried all by yourself a little bit ago."

"It didn't go so well."

"That's because you didn't have help. Guess I kept you waiting too long." She grabbed the crutches and pressed a button with her foot, lowering the bed. "Come on, swing those legs over here."

I scooted myself to the edge of the bed once again. Wendy put a crutch on either side of me.

"All right, upsy-daisy. Use the crutches to support your weight on your hands and arms, not your armpits."

Nothing could have prepared me for the burn in my ribcage. Nothing in the world.

"Make sure you're supporting yourself with your arms. It'll hurt your ribs less," Wendy said.

"Aww, our little girl is growing up so fast. Already taking her first steps." Grace tilted her head to the side, watching.

Wendy shook her head. "Ignore her."

At first, I was more unbalanced than I cared to admit. It's just a broken leg. So many people get around fine like that, but with the pain in my ribs, it was a lot harder than I expected it to be. Though, in minutes, I'd already improved.

Up and down the hall I went. It reassured me to know if I wanted to get up, I could without help.

"Okay, let's not push it. Back to bed." Wendy pointed back towards my room.

"Aw, come on. We were just going to race," Grace teased.

I giggled.

"Nope. No racing. Back to bed, Melanie." Wendy just shook her head. "Grace, you need to get to physical therapy."

"I know, I know. Always wanting to get rid of me. But just think about when I'm gone. You're going to miss me, you'll see." She smirked. "I'll be by later."

I nodded and hobbled back to my room. I had yet to make it back in bed when my parents walked in.

"Oh, honey," Mom gushed. "You're up and around. I'm so happy to see that."

Out of reflex, I smiled half-heartedly at her.

"She's doing much better, now that she has crutches." Wendy winked.

"Yeah, yeah." I rolled my eyes.

"Oh? Did you struggle at first?" Dad asked.

"Oh . . . uh . . ."

"She tried to do it without telling anyone. She took a spill, but she's just fine," Wendy finished for me.

Mom shook her head. "That's just like her, to push herself too far."

Wendy helped me shift my weight and scoot back into bed. She rested the crutches on the side of the bed. "The doctor arrived a little bit ago. I'll let him know you're ready for him to come in."

Not even a minute passed before a man entered the room. At first glance his face looked to be younger than my parents, but his salt-and-pepper hair made me question that.

"I hear you're doing so much better today." He looked at me.

"I am."

"Good, good." He looked over my chart and made a few notes, then searched our faces. "Do we have any questions?"

"When can she leave?" my mom asked.

The doctor smiled. "Ah, the most asked question of my day." He glanced back over his notes on the tablet and took my vitals. He used his flashlight, checked my eyes, and looked over the stitches on my cheek. "Everything looks good. I think we'll keep her one more night, and she can go home tomorrow, as long as everything still looks good."

"Great," Mom said. I could hear how relieved she was. "Thank you."

"Sure. Just let me know if you need anything." He gave a nod and left.

My parents' voices faded into the background as they talked about what would happen tomorrow when I got to go home.

A short time later, someone brought me lunch. A sandwich and soup. Not very appetizing. I nibbled here and there while my mom fussed over how little I ate and Dad told her to leave me alone. I finished the fruit, hoping it would be enough to satisfy her, and she didn't say anything else.

For a while, I watched my parents move about the room, opening the curtains to "let the light in," changing the water in the flower vases to "keep them fresh," and organizing the drawers of clothes.

I couldn't help wondering what it mattered anyway. It was a hospital room; it's depressing no matter how much fussing with it you do. Besides, I was leaving tomorrow anyway.

The doctor's words echoed in my head. "She can go home tomorrow . . ."

Getting out of this bed was one step closer to normalcy. Even if I didn't know what waited for me at home, it had to be better than here, where even the bed hurt.

I was lost in thought when Dad tapped my hand.

"Melanie? Are you okay?"

"Huh? What?"

"Your mom and I have a benefit tonight. Will you be okay without us here for the evening?"

"Of course." For once, I might actually have a chance to go through the books I'd fallen trying to get. "I'll be fine."

"Are you sure?" Mom asked.

"Positive."

Mom turned to Dad. "Should we take some of these vases with us so there aren't so many to take tomorrow?"

"What do you think, honey? Do you mind if we take some?"

I shook my head. "Go ahead."

After a couple trips back and forth to the car, my parents left for the night.

The light outside my window was almost gone and diminished by the minute. The books still sat on the table beside me, taunting me with their unseen pages. Not a single moment today had I been alone and able to crack one of them open without watchful eyes on me.

Grabbing the one on top, I flipped it open. A photo album. Photos of a baby—me, I assumed, with my much younger-looking parents. Pictures of my first birthday and every single one after that, ending with my eighteenth, with Jeremy smiling by my side. It was the last of the birthday pictures, leading me to believe it must have been my last.

*Eighteen.* I looked so happy.

Throughout the faces of people I didn't know, arms circled my shoulders or my waist, some of their shoulders pressed against mine.

At one point, someone brought in my dinner, and I ate while I continued to pour over the pages of my life, inspecting each picture with close scrutiny, hoping even a glimmer of recognition might pop out.

I paid closest attention to the most recent ones. One girl stood out and appeared to be in just about all of them since I was ten. Her black hair and green eyes only accentuated her beauty that progressed as time passed. Braces we both had at the same time now gone, revealing her beautiful smile, and mine.

It was weird looking at pictures, watching someone grow into a woman without knowing anything about them, like how she got that scar above her eye. I saw the stitches in one picture and found it was all I could think of. I was positive I knew at the time.

I stared at the latest picture of me and her. Where was she right now? Did my parents tell her to stay away, too?

Without notice, the book was ripped from my hands.

"What are you looking at?" Grace grinned down at the book as she flipped through it. "Who are they?"

I shrugged.

"You're staring at pictures of people you don't even remember? How depressing." She tossed it aside. "Want to get out of here for a bit?"

I glanced at the window. It was now completely dark. How long had I been studying that photo album?

"Are we allowed?"

"What are they going to do?"

I smirked. "Okay."

Grace held my crutches steady as I climbed out of bed. She rolled forward ahead of me, peeking around the corner before she rolled out of the room and down the hall, opposite the nurse's station.

"Hurry," she said.

I ignored the burn in my ribs, going at the fastest pace I could until we were around the corner and out of sight.

Leaning up against the wall, I took deep breaths, waiting for it to subside. Grace waited, watching me.

"You good?" she asked.

I nodded and pushed away from the wall.

She pressed the elevator button at the end of the hall and held it open for me to get inside.

"Where are we going?" I asked.

"My favorite place."

When the doors opened to the lobby, she turned to the right and went through a set of automatic doors that opened to an amazing courtyard completely surrounded by the hospital, like a little cave carved out inside it. It gave the illusion we were outside, yet an all-glass roof gleamed overhead.

A pond bubbled in the furthest corner, sending a small stream weaving throughout the paths in the entire area. A small bridge went over one section where the water accumulated, and large orange goldfish swam below. All types of greenery and flowers filled the area. Their fragrance permeated the large area, making it smell amazing, and fresh.

Grace rolled herself over the bridge and stopped next to a bench.

"This place is incredible." I sat down next to her, resting my crutches on the bench, grateful for a place to sit.

I was so glad my parents weren't here tonight. I never would have gotten to come here otherwise.

"I come down here a lot at night when nobody else does. Sometimes it makes me feel a little less lonely, and sometimes I come here just to think. It's quieter."

I could see what she meant. Just being here gave you a sense of peace, a tranquility the rest of the hospital didn't offer, with its looming white walls and incessant beeping of monitors.

"You know, as much as I can't wait to get out of here, I'm also scared to leave. Nothing will be the same when I get home. My parents already look at me like I'm broken; they probably won't let me do anything. I definitely won't be able to ride like I used to. It's all I've ever known, riding and competing. That's it. That's me." She looked down at the fish swimming in the pond. "I don't even know who I am without that."

"When will you be able to leave?" I asked.

"Should have already. Doctors are busy dinking around. They say they're waiting for the swelling to go down around my spine before they'll let me go. Maybe next week, they said, but they keep saying that. I stopped getting my hopes up after the second time they said it and it didn't happen."

"I'm supposed to go tomorrow."

Her face lit up. "That's great. You're going to come back and visit me, right? I mean, we're best friends and all now."

"Of course."

"I'm only kidding."

"I'm not. Technically, you're the only friend I know."

Even though she was snarky and sarcastic, she was fun and sincere, and I liked her. She had no expectation of me. No memories to pull from. She felt safe.

"Dude, you really took this to a mushy level."

I shook my head, laughing. "Sorry."

"See that orange fish right there, with the black dot on his head?" She pointed at the water.

"Yeah."

"I named him Greg."

"I like it. What about that one?" I pointed to the only one that was all orange, without any other spots.

"Oh, that's Gingy. She doesn't get along very well with Greg, so we don't like her much."

I looked at Grace, who was trying to hold in the laughter. Eye contact was all it took to break the dam, and we both laughed loudly, scaring the fish, which sent another wave of hysterics through us. My cheek burned, and my ribs ached, but I didn't care.

When we finally stopped laughing, Grace's face turned serious again.

"Have any of your memories come back yet?"

"No."

"Have you had any other visitors?"

"My boyfriend, I guess."

Her eyebrows raised. "A boyfriend, eh? You're holding out on me! Is he cute?"

My lip curled. "He is."

"Oooh, lucky."

"I don't even know what to say to him."

She put her hand up and flicked her wrist, brushing it off. "That doesn't matter. It's all about the lips anyway." She smacked her lips.

I giggled. "Well, we didn't go there."

"Lame."

"I think he's afraid of me. He was driving . . . you know. . . when the accident happened."

"Oh." She pulled her lips away from her teeth in a grimace.

"Yeah . . . everything is just so weird right now, with my parents, too. Nothing feels like me. I don't even know who I am."

"Well, I think that's the cool part."

"What? How?"

"You get to decide who you are all over again. Maybe it'll be the same, and maybe it won't, but not many people can restart their lives with a clean slate. I would love to start over and not remember. Maybe I wouldn't miss horses so much."

I took in what she was saying, and I totally got it. It made sense and partly sounded good. Another part of me worried I'd never get back what I had. Which would make me happier?

"Hey, you want to get some dessert?" Grace asked, with a twinkle in her eye.

"Where are we going to get dessert?"

"Come on." She was already almost to the door. I envied how fast she was in that thing. I glared down at my crutches.

I got up and followed behind her out of the oasis. She rolled over to a wheelchair that sat discarded by the front door. "Want to make getting around a little easier?"

"Oh my gosh, so much." I panted after the small walk.

Grace laughed at me as I tried to get the hang of maneuvering myself around.

"Let's go!" She pushed herself into the elevator and pressed number two. I rolled myself

back and forth in the elevator, practicing.

"This is kinda fun," I said.

"Give it a day," she grumbled. "Your arms will be so sore."

"Well, it beats the crutches. They should have just given me one of these from the start."

The elevator doors chimed, springing open on floor number two.

"Race ya!" Grace called as she sped out of the elevator.

"Cheater!" I shrieked, throwing the wheels forward as fast as I could, ignoring the burn.

Our giggles bounced off the walls in the hallway, echoing back at us.

Grace took a corner faster than I dared, losing me a great distance, then stopped.

"I win," she whispered and put a finger over her lips. She pressed a button, and another set of doors swung open. Bunnies and flowers covered the walls in bright colors.

"Where are we going?" I whispered. Nerves set in. We weren't supposed to be here; I could feel it in my bones.

She put her finger to her lips again, telling me to be quiet. She inched along, trying not to make any noise until we came to a galley way.

It looked like a small passage connecting the two corridors on opposite sides of the walls. Except in this hallway, there was a refrigerator, ice machine, and cabinets. Grace went straight to the fridge.

"Watch out for nurses," she hissed.

She reached inside as my heart thundered in my chest. I looked up and down the empty hallways, while she filled her lap with two sodas and gelatin cups, then went for the freezer and pulled out two popsicles.

"Go!" She was using only one hand to propel herself; the other held tight to the treasure in her lap.

We raced back to the double doors as quiet as we could. When they shut behind us, we glanced at each other, and a fit of laughter overtook us.

"Oh my gosh, my heart was racing in there!" I clutched my chest.

"Ha! That was nothing!"

At the elevator, she handed me half of the contraband and continued onto the elevator. This time, she pressed the button to take us to the top floor.

At the top, she brought me over to the end of the hallway, where an enormous window let us look down at the freeway below. For a while, we sat in silence, eating our loot, watching the cars drive by below.

"You've been all over this hospital, haven't you?"

The twinkle in her eye faded a bit. "Been here a while. Not much else to do. TV only cuts it for so long."

"Yeah. I couldn't even watch it for a few minutes this morning."

"Hey! Where are you two supposed to be?" An older woman in scrubs stood behind us, with her hands on her hips. Her scowl was intimidating, and I didn't much care for the angry way she spoke.

"Uh . . ." I didn't really know what I was supposed to say. Heck, I didn't even pay attention to which floor we were supposed to be on. I turned to Grace.

"All right, Warden. We'll go quietly." She held up her hands in surrender.

Grace wheeled herself to the elevator. I stayed close, worried this nurse would give me a tongue-lashing if I was alone. She followed behind us and into the small confines of the elevator. Our fun was over.

She even went as far as walking us all the way to our rooms. Grace turned off into a room four doors before mine. I gulped.

When I turned into my room, she kept walking. I heard her loud voice at the nurse's station, just a few paces away from my room.

"Caught some patients wandering around upstairs. They're back in their rooms now, in case you were looking for them. 301 and 305."

I couldn't hear the response.

After maneuvering myself into bed, I laid back and pulled the covers up to my neck.

Soon after, a nurse came in to check on me.

"Have a nice adventure?" she asked.

"Umm . . ."

"How's your pain?"

"I'm sore."

"I'll bet. I'll get you some pain meds. And in the future, until you're discharged, you need to let us know where you're going, in case something happens. It's a safety concern, especially with your memory loss."

I nodded.

I presumed this was what a little kid went through when they got in trouble for getting out of bed, rather than the eighteen-year-old adult sitting in the hospital bed like I was.

She brought me the medicine and turned down the lights.

"Goodnight."

"'Night," I said.

# Chapter THREE

**IN THE MORNING,** tapping woke me from a deep sleep. A bird sat perched at my window, tapping its beak at the glass. I squinted against the bright sunlight.

Rolling onto my back, stretching, I caught sight of someone sitting next to my bed. I jumped, clutching my chest.

"Oh my god, you scared the crap out of me!"

Her chortle came out of nowhere, proud of getting the best of me. "Well, I've been waiting long enough."

I groaned, rubbing my eyes. "Ugh, you're a morning person. Yuck."

"Yep, I am. And you are clearly not. It's almost lunch; you missed breakfast. Don't worry, I ate it for you."

"Thanks." I rolled my eyes.

Grace reached around the bed to press the button to make my bed sit upright.

"Hey! I'm sleeping here!" As much as I fought it, a smile crept up on my face anyway, making Grace laugh.

"Not anymore, you aren't," she said.

"Fine! I'm up. I'm up."

She stopped pressing the button, leaving me in a half-sitting, half-lying position.

"Good. I wanted to get you my number before your parents got here. They're kind of hovery."

"Hovery?" I asked.

"Yeah, you know, they hover, always watching. Sort of creeps me out."

"Oh."

"Do you have a cell phone?"

I pressed a finger to my lips. "Ah . . . I guess it broke in the crash."

Grace rolled her eyes. "They didn't get you a new one yet?"

I shook my head. I didn't know how things worked with that. Did I pay for it? Did they? I'd been too shy to ask. Not that I'd even had time to consider it anyway.

Grace grabbed the pad of paper off the counter, wrote something down, and handed it to me.

"That's my cell. You'd better call me."

"I will."

My parents rounded the corner, and my mom stopped short, like she thought she was in the wrong room.

"Uh . . . Melanie?" She peeked around Grace.

"Hi. I'm Grace." Grace rolled her wheelchair forward, with her hand extended.

It was my dad who took her hand, gently shaking it. "It's nice to meet you, Grace. I'm Ted, Melanie's dad, and this is Angie, her mother."

"Good to meet you, too," Grace said. "I should go . . . I've got therapy." She turned back towards me, raising her eyebrows. "See you later, Mel." She nodded to my parents and rolled out.

"She seems nice," Dad said.

"She is."

Mom remained quiet, her expression unreadable.

"Are you ready to go home?" Dad asked.

"I think so."

"Good."

For the next hour or so, I watched them busy themselves with straightening up my things, gathering them in small boxes, then finally taking them down to the car. The room slowly returned to the hospital room it once was, bare; much like my expectation for what my house looked like, or what kind of car I would ride home in.

When they were downstairs with the last load, the doctor peeked his head in.

"No parents today?" he asked.

"They're downstairs."

He nodded and handed me a stack of papers. "I have your discharge papers. You'll need to follow up with your primary care doctor in two days, then again a week after that. From then on, it's up to your doctor." He looked at me expectantly.

I nodded.

"For your leg, you'll need to see an orthopedic specialist in two weeks. Hopefully, if all is healing properly, the cast will come off in about five weeks."

I nodded again, this time without waiting for his sharp review.

"Any questions?"

I shook my head.

"How's the memory?" he asked.

"Nonexistent."

He glanced back down at the tablet and typed a note.

"Is that bad?" I asked.

He turned and rested himself against the edge of the bed.

"There isn't really a guide for this. With all head injuries, everyone reacts differently. I've seen it all; some remember as soon as the next day, while some it takes months, or years."

"Years?"

"That was a rare case," he said.

"But that could be me. I could be the rare case."

He shook his head. "I don't know."

My parents walked in, ending our conversation. My stomach twisted. Years? How could anyone live like this for years?

"Oh, hello, Doctor. Is everything set for our little girl to come home?" Mom asked.

"She's all set. Good luck, Melanie, and don't take this the wrong way, but I hope I never have to see you again." He winked and strutted out of the room.

"Let's get you out of here," Dad said, his eyes twinkling. He stepped over, holding out his hand to help me up.

I'd just gotten to my feet when Wendy appeared with a wheelchair.

"Hop in, Pumpkin."

She locked the wheels as I turned to sit, then pushed me down to where my dad pulled the car up to the curb. Part of me wasn't surprised to find a luxury car waiting. It shined like it just came from a fresh car wash, but I'd be willing to bet it hadn't.

I had more help than I needed getting in, arms and hands held out for me to take. I sat in the front seat, giving me more room for my cast. Mom got in behind me. The smell of rich leather almost overwhelmed me in a good way.

Dad stuck my crutches into the trunk before he clambered behind the wheel. Hints of his cologne and Mom's perfume filtered through the air, relaxing me, despite the nerves that grew more and more the closer we came to a home I lived in but didn't know.

The car stayed quiet. None of us seemed to know how to behave around each other.

Before long, the car turned into a rounded drive that sat at the base of an enormous two-story house, with four windows across both the top and bottom floors. It appeared huge for just the three of us.

I opened my door, preparing myself to get out.

I gaped at the monstrosity. "Have we always lived here?"

My dad handed me the crutches. "Since you were three."

***

I spent the better part of the first week home learning the layout of the huge house, and the rest of the time hiding in my room. Mom always seemed to be close by as I roamed, like she was watching my every move, waiting for something to happen.

*Was this normal for her?* Maybe she was trying to make herself available if I needed her.

It was clear to me now that Grace was right. The hovering was stifling.

For weeks I tried to find my place, but nothing seemed right. I hobbled around with my crutches, counting down the days till the cast was removed and the doctor cleared me to do anything I wanted. My dad was gone more often than not, working. And Jeremy kept his distance, but I could tell it was killing him. Not much I did seemed right. Even at dinner, Mom looked at me strange most often.

"What?" I asked her one night.

"Oh, nothing." Her eyes flitted to my plate.

"No, what?" I demanded.

"You don't like lima beans," she said.

I looked down at my plate, where I'd heaped a large pile of lima beans and already eaten half. "They tasted fine."

Mom nodded, her mouth set.

I pushed them to the side, unable to bring myself to eat the rest, knowing she thought it was wrong.

***

Jeremy came over at least once a week when he didn't have to work, like today. I stood, balancing on one leg in front of the mirror in my bedroom, staring at myself, trying to memorize every feature. My blue-gray eyes, which weren't overly large, though they couldn't exactly be called small either. My hair, the blonde arrow-straight locks, I think was my favorite thing about the way I looked. As I continued brushing it long after it was tangle-free, I heard the doorbell.

I knew Mom would answer it and I could take my time getting downstairs. My armpits were bruised from the crutches, and I moved as slowly as I could to save myself from the pain.

At the top of the staircase, I decided I just didn't have it in me to hobble down them again. I sat down on the top step and laid the crutches next to me. Like a child playing on the stairs, I scooted down on my butt, one step at a time, my broken leg extended out in front of me.

Jeremy, followed by my mom, appeared at the base of the stairs when I'd almost made it to the bottom. He raised his eyebrows, crossing his arms across his body. His button-up white Oxford shirt tightened against his arms.

His lips went tight as he tried to suppress a smile. "Whatcha doing?"

"Going down the stairs. My arms hurt."

He helped me to my feet. "Are you up for going out? If not, we could just stay here, like we've been doing –"

"Out," I blurted, then blushed. "Let's go out."

Jeremy turned to my mom. "Is that okay?"

"Um . . ." She paused.

"I'm eighteen. It's not up to her." I headed to the door.

I wasn't sure what transpired behind me, but I had to get away from this house. Get away from their sad eyes. I was suffocating under my parents' scrutiny. I didn't remember anything, and their constant presence was just a reminder of that.

Jeremy jogged to catch up with me. He held the car door and my crutches for me to get in.

I breathed in deep. "Where are we going?"

"You'll see."

I watched out the window as he drove, hoping to guess where we were going, but the truth was, nothing looked familiar. I may as well have been on Mars.

"I've never seen you act like that before," Jeremy said.

I sighed. *Great, one more thing I'd done that wasn't "me."*

"I didn't say it was a bad thing." He reached across the car and rested his hand on top of mine, the way he had since the accident. Maybe he always did. I couldn't say.

He stopped the car in front of a park, and I thought back to when he visited me at the hospital. He'd said, the night of the accident, we were going to a park—our park.

"Is this the park we were going to? You know, when . . ." I turned to face him.

"Yeah."

Ducks flew overhead across the bright blue sky on this beautiful sunny Saturday.

Jeremy rushed to the trunk. It took him a few minutes to finish what he was doing before he made his way around the car, pushing a wheelchair. My mouth dropped, and relief washed over me.

"Where did you get that?"

"Interning at the hospital has its perks." A small smirk revealed a single dimple.

I shook my head. "Well, I'm *really* glad."

He pushed me out by the lake and stopped. He laid out a blanket, then a bag appeared as he sprawled out.

"You hungry?" He pulled sandwiches out of the bag, as well as jalapeno chips.

"Yes. Starving."

"Your favorite," he said when I eyed the bags.

*I wouldn't know.*

He helped me down onto the ground.

"You can lean on me if you want," he offered.

But I refused and adjusted myself so my leg was straight in front of me.

I picked up a sandwich and shoved some chips inside it.

Jeremy watched me. "Some things never change."

His words should have made me feel good, but I couldn't even say why I'd done it, though it was good. Maybe some things were habits, even when you couldn't remember why you'd ever started doing them.

I watched the ducks out on the water, bobbing up and down, catching things below. The water looked so calm. If it weren't for the ducks, there wouldn't be a single ripple.

"You ever wonder if this is where you're supposed to be? Like, if you'd made different choices, would it eventually have led here anyway?"

He slid his hand across his forehead, rubbing at the center. "Not really. I mean, I've got a great life. I'm going to college in the fall. I've got the internship at the hospital. And I've got you."

"A lot of good that does when I don't even remember you."

He took my hand. "But you will. Until then, I love you, no matter what." He kissed the back of my hand and gave it a light squeeze.

His arm brushed against the scratchy cast, and his eyes roamed over it. "Did you see the doctor yesterday?"

I nodded.

"I was going to call . . . I hate you not having a phone. I always feel strange calling your house. What did they say?"

I tapped the cast. "This puppy comes off in a week."

His face lit up. "Then I guess we're celebrating!"

He reached back into the bag and pulled out two lemon cakes with red drizzle.

"Yum." I grinned.

He handed me a piece, and as our hands brushed, his face changed, serious and alluring. I didn't have to remember anything about him to know what was on his mind.

It happened in slow motion. My breath hitched in my throat as my heart raced. He moved closer and closer, his eyes slowly closing. At the last second, I turned, and his nose pressed into my cheek.

I looked at my cast, unable to meet his eye. I was so embarrassed.

"I'm sorry."

He brushed his thumb across his lips. "No." He paused. "No. I rushed you."

For a while, he focused on the water. I couldn't imagine what was going through his mind.

All I felt was pressure. Pressure to pick up where we'd left off. It wasn't him; it was me. The fear of letting him down. This was why I'd wanted to leave the house. No expectations, but I should have known. As much as Jeremy was patient, he was still human, and to him life was moving on, not paused in a place where nothing could move forward or backward.

I sighed. "I'm just not there yet."

Jeremy nodded. His face held no frustration he had every right to feel.

Jeremy was easy to hang out with. He was prim and proper in all the ways I knew my parents would love. He was very much a catch. Though, I could tell, he was very much in his own head, like he was working through his own things.

He traced his fingers over my nails.

A breeze lifted the branches on the tallest trees, tussling them around, throwing spiraling leaves around the ground.

"Should we go for a walk?"

"If you're pushing."

He helped me back into the wheelchair, cleaned up our picnic area, and started pushing me along the sidewalk.

"Tell me about some of the things we've done here."

"There was the time I tried to teach you to fish —"

"Tried? I take it that didn't go well."

"Besides hooking my arm and accidentally throwing the pole in the lake? Uh, yeah, it went great."

I slapped my hand over my mouth. "Oh my gosh. That's awful."

He stifled a laugh, and a deep rumble vibrated in his chest behind me.

"There was the time we flew kites."

"Kites?" My eyebrows raised.

"Yep. That one was your idea. It was windy all morning, so we went to the store and got some awesome ones. In fact, I think you still have yours."

I thought back. There was a kite hanging from the ceiling, in the corner of my room. It was a big blue-and-white checkered box kite.

"Why do I get the feeling that didn't go well either?"

"Oh, it was great, and then the wind died. We couldn't get the kites off the ground."

"Did we ever try again?"

"Nope."

"We should." I turned to look back at Jeremy, just to see his face. He wore a grin, and his eyes squinted against the sun. There seemed to be a relaxed sense to him, yet underneath it all seemed like he had something more on his mind.

*Probably worry, just like everyone else.*

He walked slow, taking his time with each step. We came around a bend to a niche in the trees.

"Wait, roll me over there." I pointed.

You could just barely see the pond beyond the thick shrubs and trees. The sun peeped through the canopy of leaves overhead.

"Can you see that?" I peered through the trees.

"What?" Jeremy bent, his head turning back and forth, searching.

"Come over here." I motioned next to me.

He came up beside me and knelt.

"What do you see?" He squinted.

I leaned over and kissed him right on the lips. Just a quick peck, like I was afraid of him. I stayed just in front of him, staring into his eyes. Slowly, he leaned in until his lips pressed against mine. His hand thrust into my hair at the back of my head, deepening the kiss. His touch and lips were both warm and inviting. When he pulled away, he looked into my eyes, his nose gently pressed against mine.

"This is where you told me you loved me . . ." he whispered. He backed up and looked out at the water. "What made you change your mind?"

In truth, part of me just wanted to kiss him, to feel what it was like, but another part of me just wanted the worry in his eyes to be gone.

"I don't know."

"Well, I'm glad you did." He stepped behind me again, kissed the top of my head, and started walking.

We finished our walk around the lake, and he drove me home. After he pulled into the driveway, he released his buckle and turned off the car.

"Jeremy?"

"Yeah." He turned towards me, leaving the keys in the ignition.

"Do you know what my parents do about my cell phone? Did I pay for the last one?"

He looked at me with his brows furrowed.

"I've been too shy to ask." I fumbled with the hem of my shirt.

"They're your parents." The concept of me being shy with them seemed to surprise him.

"It doesn't feel like it." I looked down at my hands.

"They buy all your stuff. Your car, too."

I nodded. *Wait, I have a car?*

"Just ask them. I'm shocked you haven't said anything yet. I think they're just afraid to share you right now. They almost lost you. *We* almost lost you. It hasn't been easy to take that in for me; I can't imagine what they must be feeling."

I nodded. "I'll ask."

"You do have your own money though . . ."

"I do?"

"Yeah. Your trust fund released when you turned eighteen. I don't think you've touched it yet though."

A trust fund? It shouldn't have come as such a surprise, with the big house and fancy cars, or with the way my parents presented themselves.

"You okay?"

"Oh . . . uh. Yeah . . . fine." I opened the door.

Jeremy rushed out and grabbed my crutches. He stood in front of me, holding my arms as I balanced on my good leg.

"I know you don't remember, and I realize how hard that must be, to wake up and not know anyone. But you do know me, you've chosen me every day for over a year now. I love you. I want you to know you can tell me anything, so if you need to talk, I'm here."

"Okay."

I could tell that wasn't what he was hoping for. The defeat in his eyes hurt, something I didn't think was possible.

He pulled me in for a hug, then backed up a little, his face hovering just in front of mine, waiting, giving me the power. I leaned forward and kissed him on the cheek.

He smiled, but it didn't reach his eyes the way I liked and had only seen a handful of times I could recall. He stepped to the side, and I could feel him watching me make my way inside.

Then his words hit me and I stopped. In the hospital, Jeremy told me it was almost a year; today, he said over.

*When was a year?*

My stomach dropped.

I whirled around. "Jeremy, did I miss our anniversary?"

His lips tightened, and he nodded.

"I'm sorry. You should have told me."

He shook his head. "Don't worry about it. When you get your memory back, we'll celebrate then."

I knew that wouldn't make it up to him, but I nodded and went inside.

My brain spun on overload. All this time, I'd been too afraid to ask about money or a phone outside of the landline, and I had a trust fund! I couldn't believe it.

I found my mom sitting in front of the bay window in the den.

"Can we talk?"

"Sure." She closed her book and removed her glasses. "What's on your mind?"

"When can I get a new cell phone?" I asked, point blank.

Her lips went tight. She stood, walked over to the desk, and opened the drawer. She pulled out a box, and something on top slid around as she walked.

She placed it in my hands and sat back down. "We were able to transfer your things to the new one."

31

"Thanks." I paused, staring at the phones; one new in the box, the other, smashed and broken, in my hand. "Why didn't you give this to me sooner?"

"You needed to rest. The phone is just a distraction."

"But isn't that my decision to make?"

She remained quiet and crossed her arms, defensive.

"What if my friends are the ones who pull me out of this? What if that's all I needed all along and you've been denying me it?"

"You've never asked for it until now."

*"Because I was too afraid to!"*

Her entire expression changed from defensive to concerned. "You were afraid to ask me for something?"

"Yes . . . I don't know you." My whisper was a harsh change from yelling just seconds ago.

"I'm your mother."

"I know you are, but you're a stranger to me right now."

She fixed her gaze on the floor, unwilling to look me in the eye.

I turned on my good heel and stormed out as fast as I could on crutches, going straight to my room.

It wasn't until later that night I even looked through the new phone. So many missed calls and texts. So many names and numbers, yet no faces came to mind.

*Feel better soon!*

*Call me when you get out of the hospital!*

*I'm so glad you're okay.*

I may as well have been looking through someone else's phone. Then there were some from Jeremy.

*I don't know if you'll get these, but I miss you.*

*Happy Anniversary!*

And then the very last one, which pulled at my heart more than I thought anything could in this state.

*I hate that you're suffering so much. I can't wait until you come back to me.*

I knew he meant my mind, my memories. My eyes burned as tears threatened their way out.

I closed the messages and tried to push them all from my mind. I scrolled through the pictures, and it seemed as though I had a very full social life. Swimming, vacations, hiking, biking, parties, and fancy events in ball gowns.

I wished I could remember even one of them.

The same girl with the scar was in almost all of them. I wished I knew her name. Then again, knowing Jeremy hadn't brought anything back; bringing anyone else into this wouldn't change a thing. One more person to feel disappointed.

I ignored all the messages and missed calls, except Jeremy.

*Thanks for today . . .*

I dug through the box from the hospital. I'd unpacked nothing in the weeks since I'd been home. Instead, I'd just stashed it in the bottom of my closet.

With the single piece of paper I'd been searching for in my hand, I looked back and forth, dialing Grace's number.

"Hello?" Her sassy voice burst through the speaker.

"Grace, it's me . . ." I paused. "Melanie."

"She lives!" She giggled to herself. "What's up? You missed me, didn't you?"

"You got me." I shook my head, unable to stop myself from smiling. She always had a way of making me smile right off the bat.

"I knew it!"

"How have you been?" I'd visited her a couple times before she got out of the hospital, but it just wasn't the same with my mom tagging along. The last time I went, she'd already gotten out.

"Fine, of course. Would you expect any less?"

"Nope." I smiled as if she were standing in front of me, then I felt silly.

"You suffocating yet?" she asked.

"Yeah, like you wouldn't believe, but I've got my phone again, so that's a start."

"I guess that still means zip on the memories."

"Uh huh."

"How's that stud of yours?"

"Good. He took me out today for the first time . . . you know, since I've been home."

"Oooh, how was that? Did you kiss him?"

I could almost picture her sitting forward in her chair, her eyebrows arched and expectant.

"Yes, and it was . . ."

"Good?"

"Yes, and weird."

"Oh." She sounded dejected.

"Yeah."

"You going to cut him loose?"

"I don't know what I'm going to do."

"That makes two of us."

"What do you mean?"

"Before the accident, I was supposed to travel and compete with my horse, but now . . . obviously, that's not going to happen."

"You going to go to college?"

"Yuck, I don't even want to think about that, but yeah, probably. Maybe to be a veterinarian."

"That's sounds great."

"Eh, second best, I guess. What about you?"

"Ah . . . I guess I got into a university in Colorado . . . but the idea of going away to school without my memory just seems. . ."

"Like a huge waste of time?" she chimed in for me.

"Exactly. I mean, I could pick a major that I like now, and then I could get my memories back and want something completely different."

"What did your parents say you were going for?"

"Business."

"Eh, boring."

"Yeah, I can't understand what I would have wanted to go to business school for."

"Maybe it's parental influence. Your dad looks like a suit."

"Maybe."

"But Colorado, huh?"

"Yeah."

"You should go anyway. The weather there is beautiful."

"And do what?"

"I don't know," she bit back with sarcasm. "Take a few classes. Get away from your parents. You know, have a little freedom."

"That's not such a bad idea."

"I don't have bad ideas," Grace said. "Think the parents will be willing to bankroll it?"

I thought about my trust fund. Just how much did I have? Would it cover me moving out on my own?

"They may not have to . . ."

# Chapter FOUR

**ONCE THE IDEA** was in my head, there was no turning back. Suddenly, all I could think about was finding my very own place . . . in Colorado. Away from prying eyes, questioning each and every move I made, like it was a symptom of a greater condition or maybe a sign I remembered something. I couldn't handle that pressure.

I searched my room from top to bottom for any information on my bank accounts, but it wasn't until I looked through the history on my laptop that I found anything useful.

What I found sprawled across three different banks would never leave my brain. The amount of zeros left circles spinning through my head. Nobody would ever know how much money I possessed. Except for Grace. I was sure, somehow, whether I liked it or not, she'd get it out of me.

Since I got my phone back, Jeremy texted me often throughout the day. I'd really grown to like him. But no matter how much time I took to get to know him, it became more and more clear to me I could never catch up. The kind of affection he had for me took time, and until I got my memories back, I'd always be two steps behind. It wasn't fair to him, but it didn't make telling him any easier.

I kept going over in my head what I'd say when the time came, but I kept worrying he wouldn't accept it for what it was—the end.

\*\*\*

My cast came off exactly five and a half weeks after the accident. Only another few days before the doctor said I could drive, and I'd be out of here. Freedom.

Somehow, I convinced my mom to drop me off at the movies to hang out with Grace. For the first time, she didn't insist on tagging along. Maybe my outburst made her feel guilty. I'm sure it helped that I could walk on my own.

Grace rolled up as soon as my mom's car swung away from the curb.

"Hey, stranger," she said.

"Hey!"

"Your keeper let you free?"

I rolled my eyes. "I'm not an animal in a cage."

"Could have fooled me."

"What movie do you want to see?"

Grace made a face.

"You don't want to go to the movies?"

She shook her head. "How am I supposed to get the dirt on all these plans you've been hyped up about if we're in a dark theater?"

I grinned. "It's all coming together."

I'd already lined up three showings and booked a week at a hotel. That only left the hard part—telling my parents and Jeremy. Truth be told, I was most afraid of telling him. I cringed at the thought. This would blindside him, I was sure, and that was quite possibly one of the worst things, never seeing it coming.

"Oooh, tell me everything!"

"I'll do you one better, I'll show you. Let's get a table." I pointed at the restaurant we stood next to.

As soon as we ordered drinks, I showed her pictures from the three apartments I'd be seeing. She turned up her nose at all of them.

"Why are you looking at such dumpy places?"

I shrugged. "They won't take much work to make them nice again."

"Yuck. Can't you just ask Mommy and Daddy to send a little money your way? Lord knows they can afford it."

"I don't need their money."

"Oh, don't be all humble. Seriously. This is the kind of thing you're supposed to ask them for money for. I mean, if it were me . . ."

"Grace, I don't need their money."

"I think you're in denial. Think about it, these places could have roaches or rats." She shivered at the thought. "Want me to ask them for you? I totally will."

"No!"

She held up her hands. "I was kidding. But seriously, if you aren't asking them for help, then what's your plan?"

"I'll get by. I'll get a job."

She narrowed her eyes. "What aren't you telling me?"

"Nothing."

The waitress came over and left our drinks in front of us. "Did you decide what you'd like?"

"Burger and fries for me," Grace said, quickly and to the point. She turned back to me, her eyes still narrowed. The momentary lapse in our conversation was not stopping her inquisition.

"Uh, can I get the lemon pepper chicken?"

"Sure, the mashed potatoes and steamed vegetables okay?"

"Yes, please."

"Okay, I'll get this in, and it should be out in a little bit."

I turned back to Grace, and her face still held the same skepticism.

"I have money. I'll be fine."

"What do you mean? How much money?"

I looked her in the eye. It was beginning to feel a little like a game of chicken. I sighed. "You aren't going to let this go, are you?"

She shook her head, her arms crossed over her body.

I held her gaze. I knew this would come. Grace was too inquisitive and to the point not to get this out of me.

"I have a trust."

"A trust? You've got to be kidding me."

I shook my head.

"I should have known. How much?"

I waited, debating if I should tell her the whole amount, or if I should just tell her how much was in only one of the accounts. I considered it carefully as I pulled my phone from my purse. I typed a number on the screen and showed her.

Her mouth dropped.

"Your parents really are loaded." She whistled through her teeth. "Wait, if you have that kind of money, then why the dumps?"

"I don't need anything fancy. I don't want anyone to know about the money either."

She shook her head. "Isn't that the appeal of having money? To be able to have nice things?"

"I just want my memories to come back. That's my goal right now. I don't need a bunch of attention. Besides, I'd rather make somewhere my own. That's the whole point of moving in the first place."

"I thought the whole point was to get away from the hovering?"

"Well, yeah. Getting to do things my way is just a bonus." I smirked.

"Look at you, taking charge and acting all adult-ish."

I put my hands out to my sides, palms up. "Someone's got to do it."

"You're leaving next week?"

"That's the plan."

"You tell anyone yet?"

I shook my head, my lips held tightly together.

She sucked air in-between her lips. "I'm glad I'm not in your shoes. I'd love to be there to see your parents' reaction though."

"Yeah, I'm waiting until the last minute to tell them. I've been secretly packing things and hiding them around my room. I'm running out of places to go with the boxes."

After my parents went to bed that night, I planned to load as much as I could in the trunk of my car, just so I'd have more room to hide things, and so I knew how much more I could bring.

Grace laughed.

"You think I'm kidding."

"Oh no, I know you're serious. That's why it's so funny."

Two steaming plates were laid before us. "Can I get you two anything else?"

"Ketchup?" Grace asked.

The waitress nodded.

Grace was not the type to eat and talk. She devoured her food like a high school football player after a game. Yet somehow, she remained clean, without a drop spilled on her. I, on the other hand, ended up with sauce dribbled down my shirt despite eating with perfect table manners, no doubt ingrained in me throughout my childhood.

"Do any of these places have a spare room?" Grace asked as she shoved the last bite of her burger in her mouth. It pressed into the sides of her mouth as she chewed.

I shook my head.

"Uh! I'm offended. No guest room for me," she pouted.

"Will a nice, fluffy couch suffice?" I offered.

She narrowed one eye. "I guess. Which day are you leaving?"

"Hoping for Thursday, the day after my doctor's appointment."

"And when are you telling your parents?"

"Monday, at dinner. And Jeremy, Tuesday night, provided I can get him to take me out."

"Cutting it right down to the wire."

"Yep. That's the plan. Less time for them to try to talk me out of it, or be mad at me, or . . . whatever it is they're going to do."

"They're going to hit the ceiling, that's what they're going to do. As for Mr. Dream Boy, I can be there to comfort him if you'd like." She winked.

"Oh my gosh."

"Man, I wish I didn't have to be here for doctors and therapy. Let me tell you, the second they say I'm okay to stop coming so much, I'm out of here. I may just join you up there."

"I would love that . . . seriously."

After paying the bill, we spent some time looking through the shops at the outdoor mall before I spotted my mom peeking through the window. Her eyes fell on me, and almost instantly her face reddened.

"Fun's over." I pointed to the window just as she disappeared towards the door.

Grace made a face and set down the sunglasses she'd been trying on.

"Melanie, it's time to come home." Mom's face was flushed, her lips pressed in a tight line.

I'd never seen her like this.

"Bye, Grace."

My mom walked with me to the car without speaking. She climbed into the driver's seat and just sat there, the keys clutched in her hand.

I buckled in and waited.

Still, she said nothing. I turned towards her, watching. Her chest rose and fell with each breath beneath her blush-colored blouse.

When she finally spoke, it startled me.

"Is there something you need to tell me?" Her voice was quiet.

My heart picked up speed. *Crap. What did she know?*

"Uh . . . no?"

"Then can you tell me why you have boxes of your things packed up and stashed in your closet?"

I winced, closing my eyes as if the verbal blow would actually reach out and hit me.

"I'm moving to Colorado."

She started the car and pulled out of the space.

She didn't say a word the whole way home, and that didn't change once we were there. Instead, she marched upstairs to her room and shut the door.

No anger. No explosion. Not even a door slam.

I didn't know what to do with this. I went up to my room and closed the door.

I had no doubt by now she'd called my dad. He seemed like the more levelheaded one, but now I wasn't so sure, not after Mom's less than zero reaction.

Pulling my phone from my pocket, I texted Grace.

*The bomb has been dropped . . .*

My phone rang almost as soon as the text sent. A selfie of me and Grace from today flashed on the screen.

"What, were you holding your phone?" I asked, instead of saying hello.

"What did they do?"

"Apparently, my mom found my boxes when I was out. I told her I was moving to Colorado. And that was it. She didn't say anything and went straight to her room."

"Whoa, I expected her to flip her lid."

"I know. I'm not even sure what to do."

"Your dad doesn't know yet?"

"Well, I'd imagine she would have called him. But I'm not really sure. I don't really have a lot of history to go on."

"Yeah, parents can be hard to figure out sometimes, when you know how they normally act . . . I don't envy you being completely clueless."

"Thanks." I rolled my eyes.

***

A few hours later, I heard a door close downstairs. I fought the urge to see who it was. Dad? Or Mom coming out of hiding?

I'd just gotten up to go downstairs, unable to fight the curiosity another minute, when a light tapping sounded on my door.

"Come in," I said.

I dropped back down on my bed, sitting on my hands.

Dad pushed the door open, at first just a crack, then all the way before he came inside and shut it behind himself.

I wished I knew what the look on his face meant. Was it worry? Was it sadness? Anger? Either way, it was clear he knew.

"Mom told you."

"She did."

I nodded, for no real reason other than to acknowledge it.

"Care to tell me what that's all about?" He planted his behind on the edge of my dresser and crossed his arms.

"I was supposed to go there for school in a few weeks anyway, wasn't I?"

He considered my question. "Yes, you were. However, your mom and I thought that since your accident . . . well, we thought it would be put off . . . until things were more . . ."

"Normal?" I offered.

"I was going to say secure, but yes, normal."

I stared down at my hands. "Secure." I said the word with disgust, testing it on my tongue, but I couldn't figure out how that applied to me. "I'm moving to Colorado. I think that's the best thing for me right now."

"You need your family right now."

"No."

He looked down on me, and I could tell he was getting upset. "The doctor said that being in a familiar place with people you knew would be helpful in drawing out memories."

"I know what the doctor said. It's not working." Frustration filled me. Why couldn't he see?

"Honey, you have to give it time."

"No. I don't. I don't want to give it time. I feel smothered. I can't even breathe here without someone taking notice." I knew I struck a nerve by the way his eye twitched.

"Your mother is just worried about you." His voice was softer now.

"I know that."

"Then why can't you just wait until you're better?" His eyes pleaded with me.

"What if I never get better? What if I spend all this time waiting around for something to happen, and nothing comes back to me? What then? I can't put my life on hold, just in case."

"Nobody is asking you to."

"Don't you see, that's *exactly* what you're asking me to do." I sighed. "I can't get my memories back if I'm constantly being watched. I feel like if I do something that's not what I would have done before the accident, I'm wrong. And I'm hurting everyone. I can't keep feeling like just living is a disappointment."

"Nobody thinks that."

"Mom does. You should have seen the way she looked at me the other night because I ate lima beans. I couldn't even touch the rest of them." I let that sink in before I spoke again. "I can't keep worrying about what move I should and shouldn't make, just because it might be different from before. This is something I have to do."

It took a few minutes before he even moved. I wondered what he was thinking. And then he came over, sat down on the bed next to me, and put his arm around me.

"I understand. I may not like it, but I understand. It can't be easy to be in your shoes. I know that, your mother does, too. If this is what feels right for you, then okay."

"Thanks, Dad." I reached up and squeezed his neck.

"All the boxes . . . am I right to assume this is happening soon?"

I gulped and nodded. "Thursday."

He stood. "Then we better get moving on finding you a decent place."

"No."

"What?"

"I want to do this on my own."

"Surely, you don't mean that. I'll check with Bruce, a colleague of mine. He handles real estate in Colorado, he'll find you a proper place."

"No. I already have showings set up."

"Okay, I'll go with you. I'll have to arrange for payment anyway." He shuffled to the door.

"No. I have to do this by myself. All by myself. My money. My choice."

"Honey, let me do this for you at least."

"No."

Disappointment crossed his face, but then he nodded and left.

Deep inside me, I knew this was right for me, but once again I disappointed someone. I couldn't wait to get out of here.

When Tuesday came, the atmosphere around the house remained cold and strained for much of the time. Dad continued being the icebreaker when he was home, though even he was more distant than he had been since the accident. I couldn't wait to escape with Jeremy; however, even there I knew it wouldn't be much better with what I had to say.

Jeremy asked me to go out tonight before I'd had the chance to ask him, making me feel slightly less guilty for what I had to do. Slightly.

The idea of adding one more person to the "Mad at Melanie Club" didn't appeal. Though I didn't really have much choice. Not really. I was leaving in less than forty-eight hours; this would be my only chance.

I curled the last of my hair when I heard voices downstairs. The sudden urge to rush down before anyone could mention a word about moving drove me out of my room.

"Jeremy," I called from the top of the stairs, captivating not just his attention, but Mom's too. "I'm ready."

He was dressed nice. Really nice. Suit nice. I looked back down over my outfit—a simple skirt and blouse.

"Ah, am I underdressed?"

"No, not at all. I had a late meeting with the hospital head. I didn't have time to go home and change."

"Oh . . . okay . . ." I glanced down again, debating if I should change anyway.

"You look beautiful," Jeremy said.

His words pulled my eyes to meet his, and I smiled, feeling reassured. His eyes twinkled as he looked up at me, and for a moment guilt pressed down on me like the weight of the world. It was hard to breathe as we walked to the car.

Jeremy climbed behind the wheel and cranked up the radio, singing along. He turned to me, smiling, and it was hard not to get swept away in the moment.

It didn't take long for the guilt to seep back in. As many times as I thought of how I was going to tell him, I'd never once considered at what point in the night. At the beginning? Give him the chance to bail? Wait until the end when he's dropping me off? At what point would be right?

He pulled the car up in front of the restaurant and pulled the keys from the ignition. When I didn't make the move to unbuckle, he stopped.

"Ready?"

Pressure to speak up like I'd never felt before made me hesitate. *Why does this have to be so hard?*

"Melanie?"

"I'm moving to Colorado, and we need to break up." I blurted it out in one breath, like ripping off a Band-Aid. That was usually better, right? Quick, and it was over.

The look on his face was something I doubted I would ever forget for the rest of my life. Like I'd just sucker punched him in the gut and stolen anything of value he'd ever had in his entire life.

If he hated me after tonight, I'd understand. I'd understand that better than I understood where I fit in to life.

"Say something," I pleaded.

"Why?"

"I can't be here anymore. I can't keep trying to be what everyone thinks I should be. The perfect mold of Melanie before the accident—I don't know who that is."

"No, I don't mean why are you moving. We've planned the move, in the fall when school started. I wasn't sure if you were still going, but . . .

why . . . do we need to break up?" His voice broke, barely above a whisper.

I turned towards him and grabbed his hand. "You've been so amazing since the accident." I gulped. "And I'm sure, before. I need to be able to go find myself, without anyone's expectations looming over me . . . including yours."

"But I don't, I don't have any expectations. None. I just want to be with you, and if you never remember what we had before, I'm okay with that."

"This relationship can't work with the thought that maybe today I'll get my memory back, or maybe tomorrow. The truth is, it may never come back, and without it, I've missed out on all the big things we've shared. I don't want to play catch-up. And it's not fair to you to always be in limbo."

"Please don't do this." He squeezed my hand as tears pooled in his eyes.

"All the love you feel for me, every bit of it, I see it in your eyes. I know it's there. I don't want you to think you've done anything wrong."

"But I did. I didn't avoid that accident."

I shook my head. "That wasn't your fault." I leaned over and hugged him as tight as I could from across the car. "Thank you for being there for me. Not just since the accident, but before too."

He held on to me for a while. His fingers dug into my back, squeezing me close. My eyes stung. When he finally pulled back for a split-second, I could see his face was tear-streaked just before he buried it in his sleeve. He sniffed, took a few breaths, and his emotion was gone.

I had to give him credit for keeping the strong front. If he hadn't, I was sure I'd have lost it.

"Can we at least still go to dinner?"

I smiled, nodding. "I'd like that."

Outside the car, Jeremy put out his elbow. I looped my arm through it, and inside we went.

Once the commotion of being seated and ordering our drinks faded away, our table fell quiet amidst the chatter around us. I tried not to focus on it, letting my eyes roam around the room, watching each of the couples and families talk amongst themselves.

"You know, we were best friends before we started dating," Jeremy said.

"Yeah?"

"Since seventh grade. The first day of school, we met in one of our classes, I can't even remember which one. When it was lunchtime, we both were wandering around the lunchroom when we found each other. Neither of us had anyone to sit with."

"So, we sat together."

He nodded. "I'd like to think we're still best friends . . ."

It wasn't just a statement. He wanted to know where we stood now that I'd broken up with him.

"I wouldn't think of you as any less." I reached across the table and put my hand on top of his.

Somehow, now that I'd broken things off, I was more comfortable around him. I no longer worried I'd do something he didn't expect. Now that we were just friends, there were no expectations. Not really anyway.

He smiled, the dimple that always stood out indented on his cheek. "Does that mean I get to come and visit you?"

"Of course. If you don't, I'll be mad."

"When are you leaving?"

"Thursday."

"Wow." He leaned back in his seat. "That soon."

I gave him a half-hearted grin.

"I don't see your parents liking that."

"And you'd be right." I laughed. "Mom took it the worst, I think. She went to her room without a word, and I didn't see her until dinner."

"Oh, man."

"She's still not really talking to me if she doesn't have to. Of course, it didn't really help anything that I didn't exactly tell her . . . She sort of found my packed moving boxes hidden in my closet."

His eyebrows rose. "And what did your dad say?"

"He was better. He talked to me about it, but he's upset because I'm doing it without his help . . . moneywise or insight."

"Your dad's a proud man."

"Yeah, he's stepped aside though. Not happily, but he has."

Jeremy nodded.

I pushed my food around my plate, though Jeremy's gaze remained focused on me.

"Can I ask you something?" I asked.

"Anything."

"Who is the girl in all the pictures with me? The one with the scar?"

He smiled. "Emily. Your *other* best friend."

I pushed the mashed potatoes to one side of my plate and took a toddler-sized bite of them.

"If she's my best friend . . . why haven't I seen her?"

"Oh!" Jeremy shook his head, his mouth full, he gulped once and continued. "She's studying abroad. Left the day after graduation. She won't be back for another two weeks or so, I think."

"Oh."

"I doubt she even knows about the accident . . . she didn't bring a phone, wanted to completely disconnect. No distractions." He paused. "If she knew, she would have been back here and at your side before you even got out of the hospital. You should know that."

I nodded. It's probably for the best. I'd be long gone before she got back.

# Chapter FIVE

IN THE REARVIEW mirror, my parents, whom I had no recollection of prior to just a few months ago, waved with tears in their eyes. Dad held on to Mom like she might fall over if he let go if even for a second. A twinge of guilt nagged at me, but I held no remorse leaving them behind.

This was it. I was heading out on my own. I couldn't say I would have planned things this way. Not even for a minute. But not having a real plan sort of excited me.

Fourteen hours was a long time to drive, but for some reason, it seemed an easy task, at least for the moment. With a couple chocolate bars in the seat next to me and the radio blaring, I felt like I could do anything.

I signaled my turn and got on the highway. I pushed the pedal to the floor and braced myself for the sharp acceleration.

My phone rang. I pressed the Bluetooth button on my steering wheel.

"Hello?"

"Melanie?"

"Yes?"

"Oh good, I'm glad I got you. It's Kerry Liz."

"Uh . . ." I drew a blank.

"Your realtor," she said.

"Ooh. Sorry."

She giggled softly. "It's fine. Are you still going to be able to make our appointment for those apartments tomorrow morning, ten a.m.?"

"Yes, I'll be there."

"Great. I added one to the list I think you might like. I'll meet you at the Brown House Coffeeshop on Third."

"Okay."

"See you then."

My stomach did a flop, thinking about getting to see some possibilities for my future.

***

Late that night, I arrived at the hotel, sleepy, starving, and on edge. Something about being ravenous really got to me, though I hadn't wanted to waste the time to stop and eat dinner.

I rounded the valet pull through and handed the attendant my keys. A bellhop rushed to the car and took my overnight bag from my hand.

"Anything else, Miss?" he asked.

"No, that's all."

I looked up at the resort and breathed in deep.

"Miss?" The valet handed me a return slip and climbed into my car, then disappeared into the lot.

"This way," the bellhop said.

"Name?" a woman with a ponytail asked at the counter.

"Melanie Avery." The bellhop waited beside me, his eyes on the wall behind me, as if he was trying to make it seem as though he wasn't paying attention.

The woman typed away at the keyboard. "Looks like you've been upgraded."

My eyebrows raised.

I'd decided before coming here that nobody would know I came from money, so an upgrade was definitely not something I'd planned. Aside from getting me here and a place to stay, my trust fund would be staying in the bank. My last splurge had been to stay at this hotel. It was one of the more fancy ones in the area. Though I'd only booked a standard king room, I intended to use all the amenities, including a daily massage. That could help my mind relax, right? Once I got my own place, there would be no time for that between fixing up it up and getting a job.

An upgrade though? Where did that put me? I'd be willing to bet it was compliments of my dad.

The bellhop showed me to my room, carrying my bag. When he pushed open the door, my mouth almost dropped. I did my best to mask my surprise and slipped him a few dollars. As soon as the door shut, I ran through the room like a child, taking a running leap and landing on the bed. It was like landing on a huge, fluffy pillow.

*Thank you, Dad!*

The room service menu caught my eye on the nightstand. My stomach grumbled, and the corners of my mouth lifted. Food.

It took only twenty minutes for my food to be brought up to my room. By then, I'd showered and thrown on my PJs. I stuffed myself in front of the TV until I couldn't eat another bite. Then I climbed into the giant bed and made myself comfortable in all the fluff.

The next morning, I plugged the name of the coffeehouse into my phone's map and headed off to meet the realtor.

She looked exactly like her picture on the website, with her perfect smile.

"How was the drive in?" she asked.

"Long."

She giggled. "I bet! Well, let's go get you a place to live!"

Immediately, I liked her bubbly and sweet disposition as she ushered me to her car.

I knew the places she was showing me would be rough, but I didn't realize how rough.

"There's one more left. The one I found just yesterday. It's a house, and it's a little more than you'd said your budget was, but I thought you might want to take a look anyway."

"Couldn't hurt." After what I'd seen today, I'd probably have to raise my budget anyway. Yuck. I didn't mind a little fixing up here and there, but not those.

"Great. It's right down the street from the coffee shop we met at this morning."

"Perfect."

My mind kept turning over the dumps we'd looked at so far, with holes in the walls the size of me and floorboards showing through the worn carpet. Oh, and the smell—I didn't even want to think about that smell in the last place. I was sure something must have died in there.

By the time we made it to the last stop, I had little hope it would be what I was looking for. Maybe I should have taken my dad up on his offer. Maybe I still would.

As if she sensed my discouragement, she patted my hand. "Don't worry, I saved the best for last. I think you're going to like this one."

Right off the bat, I knew I liked the neighborhood. I'd thought the same when I met her there that morning. The street was lined with small shops and businesses, including the cute little coffeehouse. At the end of the row of buildings sat one single house that hadn't yet been converted.

She unlocked the door and let me in first.

"The bedroom is upstairs. Through there is the kitchen. Straight ahead is the combined dining room and living room. The bathroom is over there." She pointed at a space next to a door that must be storage under the staircase.

The floors were all real hardwood and gave it character unlike anything else could. Even though they looked grungy, a good cleaning and wax, I thought, would be all they needed to make them shine like new. The walls needed repairs and paint, bad. Some were even multiple colors, like someone had been trying to decide the best colors. None of them very pretty. But on the plus side, none of the holes were bigger than a pencil.

After seeing the rest of the places, I hadn't expected to fall in love with this one, but from the moment I stepped foot inside it, I knew this was the one. This was my house.

The beautiful bay window in the bedroom overlooked the street, where I could watch people walk up and down, browsing the shops. Below the middle window was a small shelf built into the wall. A single book lay discarded on it.

*A Guide to Sewing.*

I set it back down and turned back to the realtor without a single question in my mind.

"This is the one."

***

Closing on my house took hardly any time at all since I had the cash in the bank. Part of me wished it had taken a little longer; hotel life was pretty nice. However, the other half of me was bursting with excitement of having my own space. A place to make my own.

My hand shook as I held the key up to the lock. This was my new home. My fresh start. I pushed open the door of the darkened house and took a deep breath. My lungs spasmed, sputtering against the dust.

I had a lot of work ahead of me to make this place perfect. For just a moment, I second-guessed my choice to move here.

Was having someone you couldn't remember standing over you all the time back at home really so bad?

*Yes. Yes, it was.*

Flipping on the light, I stepped inside and shut the door. My breathing was the only sound that filled the small one-bedroom house.

I climbed the stairs to the second floor, where the bedroom was, and dropped the single box I carried on the floor, sending up a wave of dust. I sighed and flopped onto the bare mattress. Home.

***

It took only a week to get my new space cleaned and unpacked. The floors didn't even need waxing—just a good cleaning, and they shined beautifully.

I'd already settled into a comfortable day-to-day schedule. Wake up. Get ready. Head to the coffeehouse. Drink coffee and search for a job on my laptop. Go home. Work on the house. Eat dinner alone and go to bed. It was a bit lonely at times, but it worked for the time being. It gave my mind the peace I'd been craving.

I'd already picked out the perfect color gray to paint the whole inside. It was light enough that the natural light complemented it, but dark enough to tell it wasn't white.

It took a lot of research online, countless how-to videos, and asking a million questions at the hardware store before I knew how to fix the things wrong with the walls. A little bit of caulking and hole putty, and they would be good as new. Most of the hardware store employees knew me by name already. I wasn't sure if that was good or bad.

It was two days into the second week of being here when I got a call for an interview. I was sitting at my favorite table in the coffeehouse. My hair was disheveled, and paint splattered my clothes. I wouldn't be surprised if my face looked similar. I'd finished painting the living room late the night before, and showering didn't seem as important since it wasn't finished.

I held my breath, listening, as I jotted all the details down, afraid I'd miss something they said.

"I'll be there," I said. It came out much more enthusiastic than I'd hoped.

I hung up, and a buzz of nerves took up residence in my stomach. This was the job I wanted most of the few I'd applied for. Assistant. Not a ton of responsibility, just something to start out with.

I picked my phone back up and dialed Grace.

"Tell me you met a boy," Grace answered without a greeting.

I sighed. "Do you think of nothing else?"

"What else is there?"

"Lots. The last thing I need right now is another boy in my life. I have one back home that I said goodbye to, and he was probably about as good as they come."

"That's different, you don't even remember him. That's messy, even if he is really cute."

I shook my head. "I got an interview."

"Oh yeah?"

"Yeah, and for the one I'd been hoping for."

"That's big! The assistant's job, right?"

"Yeah, I'm so nervous. It's hard looking for jobs when I don't remember the experience I have aside from what I've been told."

"You're going to get it. I know it."

I wished it were that simple. I thought over the questions they might ask: What makes you a good fit for this position? What would you say are your best qualities?

How did one answer these questions when your furthest memory dated back only two months, when you woke up in the hospital?

I sighed. "I hope so."

"How's the new place coming?"

"Good. It's..." I thought of the spotted walls, almost ready for paint, and the half-painted living room. I knew she'd turn up her nose if she knew. "...homey."

"Homey . . . okay. You just keep your eye out for an apartment for me. I'm coming, you wait and see."

I giggled. "Well, if I get this job, you have to come so we can celebrate. There's a nightclub a couple buildings over from me, maybe we can go there."

The distant yet still too close rhythm of the bass beats gave my pictures a nice vibration, until the club closed at three a.m.

"I'm in," she said.

"How's therapy?"

She groaned. "Why do ya gotta go there? We were having such a nice conversation."

"Sorry."

"Yeah, yeah. I should go. The dreaded thing you speak of is waiting. Call me after your interview tomorrow?"

"I will."

"Bye."

I set the phone down on the table and smiled to myself as I let the excitement for tomorrow take over. Looking up from my coffee, I spotted a pair of green eyes watching me. The smile below them lit up his face, and he tipped his head.

Nerves took over my stomach for an entirely new reason. I dropped my eyes to the table.

*Why was he staring at me?*

I looked a mess. Maybe that was it; he thought I might need help, because I looked crazy to be out in public like this.

I glanced up again. He was really cute. My heart rate picked up. I don't even know why. It wasn't like I was searching for a boyfriend. In fact, that was the last thing I needed to add to my list right now. Who would want to get involved with someone without their memory anyway? Talk about complicated.

His attention returned to me, and I looked back down at my laptop, pretending not to notice. My search for typical interview questions was on the screen. I wanted to be prepared, even if I didn't have real answers for them.

"Ahem."

My attention turned to the same gorgeous pair of eyes, attached to the man now standing over me.

"Hi, I hope I'm not bothering you by coming over like this. I've noticed you in here a few times in the last week. I figure you must be new to the area . . ."

"Oh, ah . . . yeah, I just moved here."

"I'm Jack."

"Melanie."

He smiled—his teeth were perfect, white, and impeccably straight. His black hair was longer on the top but short on the side, and you could tell he tended to finger comb it. The tousled style fit him in a way that appealed to me unlike I ever thought it would. It was quite different from Jeremy, who probably never left the house without his hair styled to perfection.

"I should let you get back to your work." He stole a glance at my screen.

I slammed my laptop shut quickly. "Okay." My voice sounded unusually high-pitched.

"It was good to meet you. I hope to see you around more." He walked away but looked back with a smirk that hit me right in the gut just as he walked out the door.

I threw up my hand to wave. It was a little over the top, though it was obvious it amused him. Then he turned and walked up the street.

*Well, that was graceful.*

***

I left the house in a rush the next day, in my most business-like pale pink dress, anxious to get to the interview early.

The office was only a few blocks away, but I didn't want to arrive winded or sore, so I drove.

My phone chimed from the cupholder.

*I hope you're doing well. I miss you.*

Jeremy.

It was the first time I'd heard from him since our breakup. Many times, I held my phone, ready to send him a text, yet no words came. Switching from a romantic relationship to friends left me wondering how to talk to him. I truly didn't know much about him and was grateful he made the first move. I waited to respond, hoping in just a little while I'd have something great to say.

As I stepped through the doors of the small office, a single desk greeted me, empty. The office was silent, and nobody was around.

"Hello?"

I was beginning to wonder if I was in the wrong place when a door opened down the hallway and a woman hustled out. Her fiery-red hair looked to be in a bun, though it was all starting to fall from its place. She carried a stack of folders at least a foot tall.

"Hi, I'm sorry. Things are a bit crazy around here right now." She dropped the stack on the desk with a *thud*. "I assume you're Melanie?"

I nodded, then second-guessed myself. *Speak.* "Yes."

"Good to meet you. I'm Cindy, I'm the office manager here. You'll probably only ever see me."

She sorted through a file cabinet behind the desk. When she found what she was looking for, she turned back around.

"I'm going to be frank with you." She paused and stopped rummaging through the file she held. "Is that okay?"

"Sure."

"I don't really have the time to interview you, nor do I have the capability to do both jobs anymore. Can you start right now?"

I hadn't expected that. I practiced my answers to all the questions last night, except this one.

"Uh . . . yeah."

"Great. Can you start by putting these in alphabetical order?"

She didn't wait for an answer and rushed away, back into the room she came from.

For a moment, I stood there, dumbfounded. *Did that really just happen?*

I walked behind the desk and set my purse down beneath it. Rubbing my lips together, I looked around the shiny room and smiled.

My first job.

The first day passed fast amidst all the files. There were so many, like they'd been piling up in a disorganized heap for weeks. Eventually, Cindy started sending the phone calls my way too, my only instruction— take down detailed messages. I never saw another person in the office the entire day.

At four p.m., Cindy came out and told me I could go.

"I'm sorry to have just thrown you in today. But honestly, you did amazing. It would have taken me forever to go through all those files and keep up with everything else I have to do." Her smile met the dark circles under her eyes. "Tomorrow will be better. We'll chat and get all the paperwork filled out. Thanks for jumping in like you did."

"Of course."

"Have a good evening." With that, she turned and walked back up the hallway to the same room she'd been in all day. I couldn't help wondering if there was someone else in there.

"Thanks, you too," I said to her back.

I decided after I was home to walk over to the diner a couple blocks away to get some take-out to celebrate. My order was waiting when I arrived: A burger; fries; and a chocolate shake. A little post-first day celebration for one.

On my way back, I checked my phone for messages. One from Dad and one from Grace, both just checking in. Then I saw the message from Jeremy, the one I hadn't taken the time to respond to that morning. I typed a quick message and sent it off to him.

*I got a job today! Hired and started on the spot!*

Then I called Grace. She picked up on the second ring.

"I got the job! Didn't even interview, they just put me right to work."

"Seriously?"

"Yeah. The place was a mess. I think they've been without office help for a while."

"Ick. Cleaning up messes. Not my idea of fun."

"Nah, it's not bad. Mostly filing. What are you up to?"

"Well, I'm at the hospital."

"What? Why didn't you say something!?"

"Well, you wouldn't stop going on and on."

"I was not going on and on!"

I could hear her laughing at me.

"Are you okay?" I asked.

"I'm fine. Better than fine. I moved my toe."

"What?" I stopped walking.

"Yeah. I'm getting scans. The doctors want to see what's changed."

"That's amazing."

"Eh. I'm not getting my hopes up. But yeah, it's not a bad thing . . . hey, I've got to go, they're taking me back."

"Go, go. Let me know what they say."

She hung up, and I had an ear-to-ear grin, thinking about Grace walking again. That was way better news than me getting a job.

As I turned the corner, someone threw open the door to the coffeehouse and ran right into me, knocking me completely off-balance. I reached out to grab the door to catch myself, but my healing leg buckled beneath me, causing me to miss the door, and I hit the pavement. My spine absorbed the impact, sending a wave of pain up and into my ribs. The air deflated from my lungs from the force. Then I heard the crackle of the Styrofoam smashing and felt the squish of the hamburger bun flattening beneath me as gravity pulled my entire body to the concrete. My shake hit the ground last, spraying it everywhere, though as I looked up, I realized the majority was on me.

*Awesome.*

My leg burned, yet the shake now coating my clothing was seeping through, giving me the chills.

"Oh my gosh. I'm so sorry . . ."

"*You*," I said, finally making eye contact. The same mesmerizing green eyes watched me, with a hint of worry.

I slipped out of my heels, leaving them to lie on the ground.

He dropped his briefcase to the ground and reached to help me up. It was then I realized not a single drop of my shake had managed to get on him. *Of course.*

"Are you okay?"

I brushed off my dress, thankful I'd worn shorts underneath, as I balanced on one foot. I hopped a few times, trying to stay upright, sending even more waves of pain all throughout my freshly healed body. Most of the shake was now just smeared around my stomach. I sucked in, trying not to let any of the cold, wet material touch me. I shoved my feet back into my heels.

"I think so." Though I feared putting weight on my leg.

"Melanie, right?"

I nodded, bending to pick up my food from the ground. I limped over to the trash and tossed it and the empty, broken cup.

"I hurt you. I'm really sorry, can I do anything? Let me replace your dinner, it's the least I can do after ruining yours."

The annoyance mixed with the temptation to get to know this beautiful man in front of me made for some very confusing emotions. I had to get away from him. He was trouble. Trouble I couldn't handle right now.

"No, that's okay. I'll just order a pizza or something."

"At least let me pay for it." He pulled his wallet from his pocket, thumbing through it.

"No. I don't need your money." I started walking away.

He shoved his wallet back in his pocket and jogged after me.

"Where are you headed? I can give you a ride. You're limping."

I stopped, frustration getting the better of me, and ground my teeth. "Jack, was it?"

He nodded quick.

"I appreciate that you're trying to make things right, but it was an accident. Equally as much my fault as it was yours." *Not really.* "I'm fine. I live right there." I pointed to the end of the row. "Right now, all I need is for you to leave me alone so I can go home and ice my leg." *And my ribs and butt.*

I spun and stalked away.

"I'm really sorry," he called to my back.

I put my hand up without turning around, shaking it twice, telling him both bye and stop in one gesture.

Later that night, after I'd found myself a new diner that delivered and the medicine dulled the pain, I thought of Jack. The sizzle of attraction was overwhelming. Each time I ran into him—usually not physically—the attraction grew. It made me nervous to think about. And angry with myself for treating him the way I had.

Where were my manners? I doubted he'd be interested in me anyway after that, so maybe I'd done myself a favor after all. Maybe avoiding him would be easier now.

I breathed in deep, and pain rippled through my chest.

I groaned, then threw back my covers and got in bed. Sleep; that's what I really needed right now.

# Chapter SIX

TODAY WAS THE first day I'd taken off since I started work. I wanted to take Friday, but Cindy said it would be busy that day and they could really use me in the office. Compromise. Thursday it was.

My staircase was finally going to get the facelift it needed. First up, sanding down the wood. I doubted I'd finish it all this weekend, but I'd sure try. The extra day would really help me get as much done as I could.

I stopped by the coffeehouse for fuel on my way to the hardware store. The warmth in the cup invigorated me as I walked.

The smell of lumber met me at the door, and I went straight to the paint counter to order another gallon of the color I needed.

While they mixed it up, I browsed the sandpaper. My stomach dropped when I spotted Jack coming down the same aisle. I bit my lip and turned away, hoping he wouldn't recognize me. Slowly, I made my way to the other end of the aisle, doing my best not to be obvious. Just as I went to round the corner . . .

"Melanie?"

My eyes fluttered closed. *Busted.*

If only I could have snuck around the corner a little bit faster. I spun around, trying to look friendly.

"I thought that was you," Jack said. "How are you?"

"I'm fine."

"Doing some sanding?" he asked.

"Huh?"

He pointed to the sandpaper I was standing in front of.

"Oh. Ah, yeah. I'm refinishing my staircase."

He let out a whistle. "That's a big job."

"Hard work is good for you."

*And it helps keep your mind occupied instead of wandering back to the fact that you don't have any memories prior to a few months ago.*

"Right you are."

I grabbed the sandpaper the video online said I needed. "I should go. I have a lot of work to do."

I turned and walked away. He walked along behind me, staying the same distance from me the whole time. It didn't take a rocket scientist to realize he was following me. I continued down the next aisle, pretending not to notice until I found the stain I liked.

When I got in line to pay, he was still behind me.

"Why are you following me?" I demanded, reaching over to grab a candy bar.

"I'm not. I need to pay, too."

I narrowed my eyes at him and spun back around.

The cashier rang up all my items and started to tell me my total when Jack interrupted her.

"Put those on my tab, Mae."

"What? No. These are mine." I tried to hand her my card. She shook her head, smiling.

She thought he was being sweet. I seethed.

"It's the least I can do for knocking you down the other day. You're still limping. Maybe you should see a doctor."

I ground my teeth together. "Not that it's any of your business, but I'm *limping* because I got my cast off less than a month ago from a broken leg."

I grabbed my things off the counter, threw down the few dollars in cash I had, and stormed out.

Who did he think he was?

"Melanie!" Jack called after me.

Picking up my pace, I made sure he didn't catch up, ignoring the stitch in my side and burn that spread down my ribs.

I was still fuming by the time I got home. Who did he think he was, butting in like that? I used the residual frustration from it in my work and got the three stairs sanded before lunch.

Maybe I did have something to thank him for. For being a huge pain in my behind. A really cute pain in my behind. Those green eyes were just so . . .

"No. You can*not* go there," I said to myself.

Now would be the worst possible time to fall for anyone. It'd be far too complicated.

It wasn't until my arm could take no more sanding that I moved to get started on the closet and realized I'd forgotten to pick up the paint.

I sighed. Time to take a break for dinner anyway.

For the first time since moving in, I took my car for something other than groceries and work. It was time I ventured out of my little two-block bubble. And maybe I'd be able to avoid running into a certain someone.

Sweaty and covered in sanding dust wasn't my typical attire for getting dinner, so I opted for Chinese take-out. I could only imagine my mom's shock if she'd seen me out in public looking this way, and it was becoming a habit, as this wasn't the first time. It wouldn't be the last.

The salty aroma of soy sauce and sweet scent of teriyaki mixed in the air and wafted to the front waiting area where I stood, waiting for my order, making my stomach growl.

"Melanie?" a woman called as she made her way out of the kitchen carrying a white paper bag filled fuller than it probably should have been for just me, but I was starving.

"Thank you." I took the bag, turned to leave, and ran right into the one person I'd been hoping to avoid. Jack.

He put his hand out and caught my food, and his other stabilized me, keeping me from stumbling sideways.

"Well, hello," he said. "We keep running into each other."

I blushed and snatched my food from his hand. "Thanks for catching that."

He looked me over. "Still working on your house?"

"Yep," I said, trying to keep this interaction as short as possible.

"Jack," the same woman called, carrying a bag similar in size to mine.

I used the moment to slip out the door. Speed walking to my car was just enough for me to get a clean getaway.

Within minutes, I was back in my driveway, my mind still on Jack. His bright smile made me gooey inside. I smiled to myself, like an idiot. What was I doing?

My phone rang, as if she knew what was going through my betraying mind.

"Hey, Grace."

"Why do you sound guilty?" she demanded.

"What? I don't," I said quickly. A little too quickly. I imagined her narrowing her eyes just the way she always did when she was on to me.

"Whatever. I'll just find out what's going on when I get there."

"There is nothing to . . . wait, get here? You're coming?"

"Yep! Tomorrow."

"Wow! That's soon!"

"Yeah, well, we've got to celebrate. I'm going to be walking before you know it!"

"*What?* Seriously?"

"Yeah, provided all the tests are right. They told me an hour ago."

"Oh my gosh. I'm so happy for you."

"You going to have room on your couch for this soon-to-be ex-wheelchair rider?"

I pictured my bare living room, aside from the floor pillow cushions and small end table.

"Ah, I'll make something work. Do you need me to pick you up?"

"Yeah. My plane gets in at four thirty-five p.m. Get ready for an amazing weekend! See you tomorrow."

"Okay!"

"Oh, and you better be ready to dish on what you're so guilty about."

She hung up before I had a chance to argue.

I glanced at my watch. Less than twenty-four hours until she would be here. That didn't give me a lot of time to get ready for her.

I changed directions and turned off at the nearest park, thankful I'd asked for silverware. Then, instead of going home after I ate, I headed off to the nearest mega store.

Two hours and four trips to and from the car later, I finished unloading all the things I'd gotten for a successful girls' weekend, the very first in my new house.

By the time I finished setting up the living room as a makeshift bedroom for Grace, I was exhausted. Feeling the pull of gravity on my eyelids, I glanced at the clock—eleven o'clock. I yawned. Time for bed.

***

First thing the next day, I walked in to work and got settled at my desk. Just like every other day, Cindy had already disappeared into the back office, where I knew J.R., the owner of the company, was, and my desk was already piled high with files. How they went through so many files each day was beyond me.

I'd only worked there a short time, but I thought it was odd I'd still never met my real boss, and he didn't seem to mind since he never made a point to introduce himself. As busy as Cindy was all the time, it didn't surprise me he was in the office before me and left after. But part of me wondered if there was another exit from his office. That would ensure I would probably never meet him.

I was pondering this when J.R.'s office door opened and Cindy strutted out. She carried a stack of files, like she often did.

"Good morning."

"Morning," she breathed. "He's in a mood today."

"Oh?" I debated if it was a bad idea to ask to get off early. I watched her sort through things. "Uh . . . I know you said today would be busy, but would it be all right if I left a little early? I have a friend coming in town, and her plane gets in at four thirty-five. It was sort of a surprise."

"Sure," she said without looking up from what she was doing.

Then she turned and disappeared back in the office. It was rare she worked anywhere else. I set an alarm on my phone so I wouldn't lose track of time and settled back into my chair to start organizing the load of papers and files that had been stacked on my desk.

When my alarm went off, Cindy wasn't around as she usually was when I left. I hesitated for a moment, wondering if I should go back and say goodbye. Instead, I scribbled a note to her and left it on my cleared desk before grabbing my things and heading out the door.

I practically skipped to my car, more than ready for the weekend.

Grace was waiting at the curb after I circled the airport for the fourth time. I jumped out, threw her bag in the trunk, and topped it off with her wheelchair once she'd lifted herself into the passenger seat.

"How was your flight?"

"Eh, wasn't bad, got on and off first because of that thing." She pointed towards her wheelchair in the back of the car. "And a cute guy helped get my bag, not that I needed it." She winked.

I laughed. "Of course."

"What can I say? I like boys."

The ear-to-ear grin didn't leave my face as I shook my head.

"Now, what are we going to do tonight?" Mischief sparked in her eyes. "I searched your address online and found a club that's right down the street from you."

"Yeah, that's the one I mentioned. I never checked if they allow under twenty-one though."

"They do." She smirked.

We grabbed a pizza on the way back to my house.

She looked around my half-finished house with a curled lip. "You know you have a trust fund, right?" Sarcasm hung on her words.

"I like fixing it myself. It's been . . . fun."

She shook her head. "It's a good thing I'm here, then. You need to get out."

I thought about my daily routine. I even had one on weekends. None of which included seeing friends or going out. I hadn't even tried to make friends yet, I'd been putting it off. Somehow, "Hey, my name is Melanie, I have no memories prior to a few months ago, what's your name?" just didn't seem like it would win me many takers.

"Yeah, I guess you're right."

"Of course I am." She shook her head, like there could be no other answer.

I finished off the last of my first slice of pizza and grabbed another. "So, tell me about this stuff at the doctor's."

"There's not much to tell. They kept me in the hospital so long to reduce the stress on my spine in the hopes that no more damage would be done, and I guess it worked because once the swelling really started to go down, I started getting sensations down my legs. They think it's my nerves reactivating."

"Wow. So they think you'll walk again?"

"Yep, that's what they say. And look." She pulled up on her pant leg, exposing her foot resting in a pair of black flip flops. Her big toe wiggled.

My jaw dropped. "That's amazing."

"I know. It's still a long ways out, but it's something."

"Heck yeah, it is!"

She smiled, and this time there wasn't any snarkiness behind it. It was filled with genuine happiness.

"When should we go tonight?"

"The club opens at eight. So, maybe nine?" she suggested. "We don't want to get there too early."

I nodded.

"Do you have clothes?" She looked over my outfit.

"Yeah."

"I mean clothes that aren't . . . fit for tea."

I rolled my eyes. "These are my work clothes."

"Okay, well, I need to see your outfit." She pointed upstairs towards my bedroom. "Go put it on and show me."

"Fine. You'll see. I have cute clothes," I called over my shoulder.

But as I mounted the half-sanded steps, I recalled my entire wardrobe in my head and began to doubt I had anything she'd like.

I flipped through my entire closet before I came to the one thing that may work. A simple black dress that hung to my knees. It was loose-fitting, and with my longer hanging necklace, I thought it would be fine.

Grace took one look at me and scoffed. "Really? That's your best *club* outfit?"

I shrugged. "Looks good to me."

"You look like you're going to a funeral."

"I do not!"

"It's a good thing I brought you an outfit."

"You what?"

She rolled herself over to her overnight bag and pulled out a dark denim jean jacket and white crop top. "You do have skinny jeans, right?"

"Yes."

"Good, then all we have to do is your hair and makeup."

"Wait a minute, what about you?"

"Oh, trust me, I'll look amazing when we leave here tonight."

And she did. Heads turned in our direction the entire time we made our way to the front door of the club. I squirmed under their scrutiny, but not Grace; she seemed to enjoy the attention.

"Everyone's staring," I whispered.

"That's 'cause you look hot."

My cheeks burned. "Wait, aren't we supposed to wait in line?"

She waved me off and wheeled herself forward. I jogged to keep up with her, my heels clicking on the pavement.

The bouncer at the door took one look at her and waved us through. I looked at her in awe. "How did you do that?"

"It's a gift."

I shook my head.

We weaved our way through the crowd. The deeper we went, the louder the music became until the room opened to a huge dance floor. The bar on the right was lit with LEDs that changed and flashed with the music.

Grace made her way to a table right next to the dance floor and turned herself around to watch. I sat down beside her, and before long a waitress came over.

"Hey ladies, can I get you two something to drink?"

"Uh, just a soda water for me."

Grace gave me a look. "Soda water?"

I shrugged.

"Can I get an Italian soda? Raspberry?" Grace asked.

"You got it." She walked away, her hips swishing back and forth. I'd bet that very move earned her some hefty tips.

"All right, so what's your type?" Grace rubbed her hands together.

"You're not fixing me up."

She rolled her eyes.

"I'm serious. I don't need that kind of complication in my life right now. That's why I ended things with Jeremy, remember?"

She turned to me. "Funny, I thought you ended things with him because you thought he was further along than you and that made you feel awkward. And then there's the whole long-distance thing."

"Well, those reasons, too."

"Nobody is saying you have to get married, or even get into a relationship. But you can dance, and even date. Come on!"

"Fine."

"So, you like 'em like Jeremy, clean-cut? Or would you like someone more grunge . . . or maybe you're more in-between," she mused, scratching her cheek.

I considered her options. "In between, or like Jeremy, I guess."

"Got it. Give me five minutes." And with that, she rolled away into the crowd.

I opened my mouth to ask where she was going, but there was no way for her to hear me. The waitress returned as soon as Grace left my view. She set the drinks down on the table, and I handed her some cash, enough to cover the drinks and a tip.

"I'll be back to check on you guys in a bit."

I nodded, and she moved on to the table beside me.

I absently bounced from side to side in my seat with the beat and watched everyone dance around me. I couldn't help noticing a few guys out on the dance floor were really attractive. And I started to come around to this dating idea. I mean, people casually dated all the time. Nothing had to come of it, right?

"Excuse me?" One of the cute guys I'd been admiring stood over me. Light brown hair, huge brown eyes, and perfectly tanned skin. Yep, he looked good.

"Yeah?" I expected him to ask for the spare chair, or something else.

"Would you like to dance?"

I smiled up into his brown eyes and found myself saying, "Sure," without even a second thought.

"What's your name?" he asked over the loud music as we danced.

"Melanie. What's yours?"

"Ben."

I nodded, turning my back to him as I danced, to look around for Grace. *Where was she?*

The song slowly changed into another as the DJ mixed in the booth.

"Are you from around here?"

"Ah, I live just up the street." I stopped myself from pointing, since I didn't want to find an unwelcome visitor I'd just met on my doorstep.

"Cool."

I found myself suddenly unable to think of anything to say, not just because I was competing with the music, but because I'd suddenly found Grace. She was making her way back over to the table with the one person I'd never expected her to find. The one person I'd kept running into and found myself thinking about way more than I should. The one person I feared I couldn't resist much longer.

Jack.

He wasn't alone. At his shoulder, another guy tagged along. He was a little bit shorter than Jack, but he made up for it in bulkiness. His muscles bulged, like he was a full-time bodybuilder. *Of course.* It wasn't hard to see she intended Jack for me.

Maybe if I kept dancing, she'd send him on his way. I scooted closer to Ben. Maybe she'd approve. But when the song ended, she waved me over and I cringed.

"Thanks for the dance," I said and made my way back to her, ready to tell her I wasn't interested, but she cut me off before I started to speak.

"Melanie, this is Jack and Alex. Guys, this is Melanie."

I turned to Jack, who smirked. "We've met."

My eyes didn't leave Jack. "It's good to meet you, Alex."

Though when Alex didn't respond, we both turned to Alex and Grace. They'd completely tuned us out. I doubted they'd heard anything we said.

"Oh my gosh." I shook my head.

Jack chuckled. "Alex tends to have that effect on women."

His smile ignited something inside me, something I'd been trying so hard to smother. Even now, with as much as I tried to fight the draw to him, I couldn't. I wanted to tell him to leave, that I didn't have time for dating, but the words wouldn't come. Instead, I found myself focusing on his arm brushing mine.

"Can I get you a drink?" Jack asked.

I picked mine up from the table. "Got one."

"Great, everyone has drinks. Mel, I'm going to show Alex how to really take a girl around the dance floor."

I stepped to the side as Grace wheeled herself through, with Alex in tow. She spun herself in a way I didn't know wheelchairs could even move, bobbing her head and body from side to side.

"Okay . . ." I wanted to kick her for leaving me alone with him.

"It's good to see you again. Without running into you, I mean."

I nodded, sipping my drink. I looked around, doing my best to keep my eyes busy, away from the gap in his shirt that made me want to keep looking down to see what was underneath. I shook myself. *Stop it.*

"This isn't really your thing, is it?"

"The music's good."

"In other words, you're trying to like it, but the music and your friend over there are the only things keeping you here."

I pursed my lips. "Pretty much."

He leaned over. "Me, too. What do you say we go for a walk? I think they can keep each other company for a while."

I watched Grace. She was laughing hysterically, her head tilted back.

I should have said no and not let myself go further than sitting here talking, as Grace expected me to. Something told me if I let myself be alone with him, I'd like it. A lot. How could she have picked the one guy I couldn't stop thinking about?

"Okay." I sipped the last of my soda water and stood, giving Grace a wave.

She fanned her hand, telling me to go, and mouthed, "Have fun."

I took the lead and headed outside. The loud music faded behind us, yet the bass still vibrated the ground, much like it did my walls at home.

"Coffee?" He pointed towards the coffeehouse two doors down.

"Isn't it closed?"

He reached into his pocket and pulled out a key.

"What? How do you have a key? Do you work there or something?"

"Something like that."

"Well, then sure."

He unlocked the door.

"Ladies first," he said, holding the door open for me.

He locked the door behind us and flipped on the light. "What would you like?"

"A decaf white mocha?"

"Coming up. Go pick a table." He went behind the counter, and I could hear the steam hissing.

I made a lap around the dining area before I sat down at the table by the window, the one where I always sat. He came over and set two steaming mugs on the table, along with a plate of biscotti.

"Ooh, the warm mug." I spread my hands around it, letting the warmth defrost my cold fingers.

"Best part, right?"

I nodded. "Hands down."

"You really like this table, don't you?"

My lips curved up. "I guess so. It's the best view of the street." I grabbed a biscotti and dunked it into my coffee.

"So, what made you decide to move here?"

I shrugged. "Why does anyone move anywhere?"

"You know what I mean. It's a small town. Not exactly a big city."

"I needed a change. I was supposed to go to school about thirty minutes away."

"Supposed to?"

"Uh, well some things happened, and I haven't decided if I'm ready to start that just yet. Kind of late now. Maybe someday."

"I see."

I could see he wanted to ask more, like what would cause someone college bound to completely change course and not know when she would start again.

"What's the story with this place?" I asked. "Something tells me you don't just work here. You the manager or something?"

Leaning forward on his arms, he eyed me. "Something like that."

"You aren't going to tell me?"

"Nope."

I laughed. "Why?"

"Because I like to be a little mysterious. Besides, I couldn't lay all my cards out on the table without knowing much about you. How would that be fair?"

"Fine. What do you want to know?"

"What were you going to go to school for?"

I made a face. *Back to that.* "Business."

"Really?" His eyes grew larger.

"Yeah."

"I guess you are full of surprises. I never would have pegged you for business."

"Oh yeah? What would you have pegged me for?"

He sat back in his seat, considering this. I waited, eyeing him.

"Nurse, or maybe a doctor. We should probably add contractor, with your trips to the hardware store. Sounds like you've been there a lot."

"What? Who said that?"

He grinned. "The cashier, after you stormed out."

I shook my head.

"Small town, remember?"

Neither of us spoke for a while, drinking our coffee and letting the distant bump of the bass at the club lull us.

"How's your leg? I didn't see you limping tonight on the dance floor."

"Oh, it's fine."

"How'd you break it?"

"Ah." I eyed him.

"What? Is it a big secret?"

"No, not exactly."

"Well . . ."

"I broke it in a car accident."

"Oh, ouch. Must have been a bad one."

"It was."

"That have anything to do with why you moved out here?"

I looked him in the eye. "Wow, we're getting deep already."

"Am I? Sorry, you don't have to answer that."

I downed the rest of my coffee and stood. "This was . . . nice, but I should probably get back to Grace."

"Wait, let me walk you."

Leaving everything where it was, he unlocked the door and shut off the lights before locking the doors behind us.

"I hope I didn't offend you." He shoved his hands in his pockets.

"No, you didn't." *You are just getting too close. Way too fast.*

"Good." We walked back into the club, once again without waiting. This time, the line had disappeared. Either people had decided to go elsewhere, or there weren't that many people to begin with.

When we stepped inside, I could tell right away it was way busier than it had been before. Everyone was shoulder to shoulder, dancing, not just on the dance floor, but all around the room. A few girls stood on the bar, dancing in skimpy clothes.

"Wow, it filled in quickly."

"Always does," he shouted back over the noise. "Want to dance?"

"Sure." Couldn't hurt now that talking was next to impossible.

We jumped in next to Grace and Alex. Jack was a good dancer. A really good dancer. But he took me along with him, and I found myself having more fun than I'd had in a long time. He didn't coddle me like I was broken. He wasn't even gentle as he swung me around the dance floor. A few times, I felt the distant ache in my ribs, but I ignored it.

At one point, he pulled me backwards into his body. I could feel the sway of his hips as he pulled me against him. I never knew how good someone's hands could feel resting on your flesh. I reveled in that moment, his warm breath on my neck. I yearned for him to press his lips to the tender skin at the nape of my neck.

And then he grabbed my hand and spun me. It was the jolt I needed to snap me out of the spell.

"I should get home." I turned to Grace. "I'm getting tired. Are you ready to head out?"

She flashed me a pouty lip and turned back to Alex, handing him her phone.

Jack refused to let me leave without at least walking me to the door. "Can I get your number?"

I hesitated. Maybe it would be best to leave this up to fate. As much as I'd run into him, I didn't doubt there would be another time, and if there wasn't, I'd be out of this predicament. "If we see each other again, yes." I smirked up at his surprised face.

He recovered quickly. "I look forward to it."

He waited there until Grace joined me, then said his goodbyes.

The whole way back to my house, she gushed about how amazing Alex was. All the while, I remained quiet, trying to dissect my feelings towards Jack. And thankfully, Grace never asked.

*** 

The next morning, my eyelids fluttered open just briefly and found Grace staring at me. It was all too familiar. I flashed back to the hospital and beeping monitors.

"Ugh! I forgot. You're a morning person." I threw my arm over my face.

"Wake up! Wake up! It's time to get up." Grace shook me.

"No! Go away."

She changed tactics and started tickling. Giggles erupted involuntarily.

"Savage!" I squealed, rolling off the bed to escape her onslaught. "There. I'm up! Happy?"

"Yes, because *you* have to take me to the airport."

"Already?"

She nodded. "Therapy in the morning. And I've got a date."

"You planned a date for when you get back?!"

"Sure did, why not? He's really cute."

I shook my head. "I don't know how you do it."

Then I thought of Jack, and butterflies filled my stomach and my excitement to see him again grew. I couldn't say if I'd ever felt this way before, but if all guys gave Grace even half this feeling, I could sort of understand. Just a little.

Thirty minutes later, I left her at the curb in the hands of an airline assistant. Grace's face when the guy's crack slid into view when he bent to grab her bag was priceless.

I hated that she was already gone. It made my house feel so empty. Not even twenty-four hours with her. On the plus side, I'd have some time to work on my staircase.

# Chapter SEVEN

**I WALKED INTO** work Monday morning with a bit more pep in my step. The short time this weekend with Grace had been exactly what I needed to feel revitalized. But if I was honest with myself, I knew a lot of it had to do with Jack. He'd given me a lot more to be excited about than Grace had. *He* put the butterflies in my stomach.

I put my things under my desk like I always did and started to tackle the enormous piles of files on my desk. They'd stacked up way more than usual and overflowed to stacks on the floor. The boss must have been working through the weekend.

Cindy came out shortly after I arrived, with another stack.

I raised my eyebrows. "Looks like you guys emptied the file cabinets over the weekend."

Cindy rolled her eyes. "There's no *we* about that." She pointed back towards the office. "He did."

"Wait, seriously? I was kidding. All of them? They're as tall as me!"

She nodded. "You should see his office." She turned and headed back, only to return again with another stack, which she added to the three already on the floor.

"Hey, is there any way you can stay late today? He's really wanting to go through everything and get rid of what isn't needed, but I just can't. I have a dinner party tonight. If he'd have told me earlier . . ."

"It's fine. I can stay. It's not a problem."

"Really?"

I nodded.

"Great! You're saving me!"

She hurried off back to his office and disappeared just as the phone rang.

"Hello, thank you for calling J.R. Unlimited. This is Melanie."

Four o'clock seemed to come quicker than normal, with my head buried in file cabinets. And my desk still looked full.

Cindy stepped out of the office, saying goodbye, her purse slung over her shoulder. "I'm out of here. Thanks for staying. I owe you one."

"Sure. See you tomorrow."

She gave one last nod and left, leaving me alone with my boss, who I'd still yet to meet. The nerves in my stomach simmered. I couldn't help my wandering mind. What would he be like? Old and gray? Young? Grouchy? Couldn't be too grouchy if Cindy liked him—she was too sweet to take any crap from a grouchy old man.

Was I expected to go to the office to help, like Cindy, or did he just need me here to put it all away?

I stood there, trying to decide while I thumbed through the next stack, when the door opened again. My eyes followed the light in the hallway, waiting for someone to emerge. With a trash bag slung over his shoulder, J.R. emerged. I couldn't yet see his face, hidden behind the bag.

He walked closer to my desk, and when he'd almost reached me, he bent over, dropping the bag, and stood.

My mouth hung open, and a smile formed on his face.

"*Hey*," he said, recognition evident.

I clamped my mouth shut. "*You* . . ."

"Yes, me." Jack chuckled. "I guess fate would have it, then."

*No.*

I suddenly felt like I'd been deceived. Like he'd known the whole time and intentionally didn't come out to meet me until I'd already grown to like him. More than like him. Grown to see myself dating him. To hope that someday . . .

"Did you know?"

His face changed to confusion. "Know what?"

"Know that I worked here. Did you know it was me? All those times you ran into me . . . this weekend . . ."

He laughed nervously. "What? No. Of course I didn't."

"You were so friendly." I dropped into the chair at my desk. "What was all that? Like some kind of game?" I couldn't understand what he had to gain.

"It wasn't a game. I was just trying to be friendly."

"You said your name was Jack . . . not J.R."

"Yes, I did. For personal matters, I go by Jack. J.R. is a lot more . . . I don't know, just less personal." He seemed almost annoyed to have to explain his name choices. Almost.

"Oh." I pressed a finger to my temple.

He stood there for a second longer, then bent, grabbing the trash bag again. He hefted it to the door, where he stopped, leaning back inside. "You know, it's kind of funny." He smirked, and the door banged shut.

I breathed out. *What the heck just happened?*

When the door opened again, I sprang up on impulse and grabbed a stack of files I'd already organized, then began stuffing them back in the cabinet.

J.R. . . . Jack . . . I didn't even know what to call him now, stopped behind me. I could feel his piercing green eyes at my back.

I turned back to him once they were all in. "So, what is it you need me to do tonight? The usual? Or something else?"

"I don't feel much like working anymore," he said.

I opened my mouth to speak but shut it again when no words came.

"What do you say we go get dinner?"

"Ah . . . I should really finish this." I motioned to the desk more than half-covered with files and papers.

"I think your boss will be okay if they stayed right there until tomorrow."

I sighed. "I don't want you to get the wrong idea, but I can't date anyone right now." I kept looking from him to the wall behind him as I thought of how excited I'd been about my time with him this weekend, and now . . . there could be nothing between us. Ever.

I should have stuck with my original plan and not let Grace talk me into this, into wanting more, before my life had more . . . stability. More certainty.

"Why?"

"For so many reasons . . . but let's just go with, you're my boss."

"Cindy is your boss."

I cocked my head to the side, rolling my eyes.

"She is. You hadn't even seen me before today. Surely, for me to be your boss, I would have had to meet you before now."

"Who writes my check?" I challenged further.

He smirked. "Cindy."

"Fine. Who pays it?"

His lips tightened. "Eh, specifics. Nobody cares about that."

"I do."

"Why?"

"Because I can't date someone who's paying me."

"Fine. I'll pay Cindy extra, and she can decide how much to give you."

I shook my head. "That's the same thing."

"Is it?" He rubbed the stubble on his chin, and I thought of his breath at my neck as we'd danced at the club.

My mouth went dry. I gulped, nodding.

"Fine. I'll order takeout, and we can work." He made a face, sticking out his tongue, and pointed his thumbs down. "No date . . . today." He turned and disappeared in his office, for once keeping his door open.

I went back to working, cursing myself for being stupid enough to get hung up on him. I knew how hard it was going to be to get my mind off him and his amazing green eyes.

Without Cindy there to pile more on, I got through the stacks quickly. For a few minutes, I stared at the empty desk, trying to work up the courage to go back to his office. I pictured him sitting at a desk like mine, towering with files, but when I stepped inside, I found his office to be much bigger than the rest of the whole place. Inside, he had an elliptical machine, mini fridge, couch, and a TV even hung on the wall. There was even a smaller version of his desk in a corner—I'd guess it was Cindy's. His desk was clear; behind him, however, was loaded with piles of different things. As I suspected, there were two doors in his office; a bathroom, and one that looked like it went outside.

"Can I help with anything?" I asked.

He looked up as if he hadn't heard me enter. "You finished all that out there?"

"Yeah."

"Wow, you are fast." He looked around his office. "Not yet, but the food should be here soon. Hope salads are okay?"

I nodded.

"You can come in," he said, motioning to the chair across from him. I rubbed my palms on the front of my dress slacks, wiping away the nervous moisture.

He closed the file he was working on and checked his phone.

"Be right back."

He returned moments later with two takeout containers. He set them both on the desk and pushed them towards me.

"Pick which one you want."

One appeared to be Caesar, and the other, some kind of mixture of veggies and what looked like ranch. I took the latter. I looked up to find him watching me.

"The whole fish in the dressing weirds me out."

He laughed. "You can't even taste it."

"My stomach *knows*."

"Good to know." He popped open the fully stocked mini fridge and pointed. Between sodas and coffee drinks to flavored and regular water, I pretty much had my choice of anything.

"A water bottle, please."

He tossed it to me and took one for himself.

"You've got quite the setup here."

He looked around. "Took about a year, but I think I finally have everything I could ever need." He chuckled, looking at the TV. "And more."

"It appears that way," I said. "So, I have a general idea, but what exactly do you do with all these companies?"

"What do you think I do?" he asked with a smirk as he pushed another bite into his mouth.

*Ugh. I hope I don't guess wrong.* "Do you manage businesses? Like, their books?"

"Close."

He went on eating. I waited, but it became clear he wasn't going to elaborate.

"Are you going to tell me?"

"Eh, I think I'll save that for our next date."

"What? This isn't a date."

He smirked. "*Okay.*"

"It's not."

"Whatever you say."

I shook my head. Deep down, my stomach flopped.

*Stop it.*

I was in trouble. Those green eyes; they were trouble.

Big trouble.

He took a sip of his water, still smirking. I couldn't stop my mind from wandering back to this weekend. To Jack. To the fact that all this time I'd been trying to avoid him, there I sat, just feet away from him every day for weeks, working for him, and yet neither of us knew.

"Can I ask you something?"

"Shoot." He pushed the last bite of his salad into his mouth and shoved away the empty container.

"Why didn't you come out to meet me?"

He laid his hands across his stomach and looked at me. "I don't like many people knowing who I am."

My brow furrowed.

"Sometimes, people get ideas about me . . . and about my money. Sometimes, that's all they see, and they try to take advantage. It happened with my dad all the time, and me too, as I grew up. My friends saw the money I came from and thought that entitled them to some of it. When I started my company in a new town, I saw that as a chance to start over, to change that cycle, if you will. I chose to separate myself from it the only way I knew how."

"So, that's why the Jack . . . J.R. thing?"

He nodded. "Everyone around town knows me as Jack. And nobody has seen J.R., except Cindy . . . and, I guess, now you."

I finished the last of my salad. I completely understood his point. We had a lot more in common than I realized. We both were pretending to be something else for fear that people would act differently around us because of our money.

My heart fluttered. In that moment, I questioned whether I could stop this. It seemed like an unstoppable force was pulling us together.

*Fate.*

Never in a million years would I have expected that little word to come back in such a big way.

I gazed up at him, his eyes fixed on a sheet of paper, and something happened within me, making me question whether I even wanted to stop it anymore.

I gathered up our containers and left the room, needing a minute to myself. Tossing them in the trash under my desk, I grabbed my purse. I searched for my gum and popped a piece in my mouth, took a deep breath, and headed back.

"Are you finished with any of these?" I pointed to the piles behind his desk.

He stood without speaking, bent at the knees, and lifted the biggest stack.

"I can get those . . ." I said.

He brushed past me and set them on my desk.

"Thanks."

He nodded and headed back to his office without a word. He seemed to be in the middle of a deep thought, so I let him be.

The stack was far larger than any Cindy ever brought me. I doubted she'd have been able to carry it. But I tackled it like I would any other.

I don't know if it was the late hour or preoccupation of my thoughts, but it seemed to take longer than normal to get through them. The last few files were in my hands when the light down the small hallway went out. With a messenger bag slung over his shoulder, Jack . . . err, J.R. emerged.

"I can't look at another file tonight. My eyes are starting to cross," he said. "You almost finished?"

"Yep. These are the last of them."

I took a moment and sorted them throughout the file cabinet. He watched, waiting. I slid the last drawer shut and turned to grab my things, hoping not to make him wait for me longer than he needed to.

He stopped at the door, holding it open for me, then flipped off the lights just as I slipped through.

"Have a good night," he said. "I don't expect you in tomorrow until at least eleven o'clock."

"Okay."

I headed straight to my car, leaving him behind to lock up. My doors unlocked with a touch of the button, yet for some reason my dome light didn't come on. I didn't think much of it until I pushed my key into the ignition and turned. Nothing happened. I tried again with the same result.

*Crap.*

I tried to turn it over one more time and was again met with silence—not even a single *click*.

I glanced in my rearview in time to see lights flicker on across the parking lot. I got out and popped open my hood. More than likely, it was a dead battery. I checked my trunk, but I already knew I didn't have jumper cables.

*Shoot!*

Jack pulled up beside me. "Something wrong?"

"Ah, yeah, my car won't start. I think it's a dead battery. You wouldn't happen to have jumper cables, would you?"

He shook his head. "I do not." He got out of his car, leaving it running, and climbed behind the wheel of mine. His cologne followed him as he brushed past. I closed my eyes, breathing it in.

*What are you doing? "He's your boss!"* I mouthed to myself.

"Nice car."

I absently looked over the luxury car my parents bought me. My eyes settled back on Jack, and his eyebrows raised. I blushed.

"Oh . . . uh . . . thanks."

He nodded and turned back to the steering wheel. I probably looked like a crazy person. I didn't expect his eyes on me.

He tried turning it over, with the same result as before. I stood there watching as he walked around to the front and shut the hood. He pressed the lock button on the door and handed me the keys.

"I'll give you a ride home. We can take care of this in the morning."

"We?"

"Unless you have another ride back here in the morning?"

I wanted to say I did. "No, I can walk."

"Nonsense. Get in." He walked around to the driver's side and waited for me to get settled before he pulled away.

His car smelled exactly like his spiced scent mixed with leather. Never would I have thought anything mixed with the strong smell of leather would smell this good, but it did.

"Where to?"

My stomach didn't seem to know how to feel sitting this close to him. It wanted to lurch with excitement, but then somehow it would drop again with the realization of how complicated this could be.

"Go to the coffeehouse. My house is on the other end."

"On the same strip? With all the businesses?"

"Yep."

"I didn't realize anyone had bought that place. Pretty rundown, isn't it?"

"It was. Not so much anymore."

"Right, the hardware store. Are you doing all the work by yourself?"

"I am."

"Wow. She's good with filing, phones, *and* construction. A woman of many talents."

I laughed. "The Internet can teach you anything."

"How very true. You'll have to show me all the work you've done sometime. I might have a thing or two to learn from you."

"Ha! I don't know about that."

For a few minutes, the only sound that filled the car was the occasional blinker click. My stomach twisted a little tighter, feeling the pressure to say something. Anything.

"Can I ask you something?"

I breathed a sigh of relief. Silence broken. "Sure."

"Do you have a boyfriend?"

"What?" I turned to look at him.

"Well, I have to know if that's why you're so against a date."

I turned away fast to avoid him seeing the smile that deceived me. The flutters were back, tickling my overly stimulated insides. "No. I don't."

"But really, what is the reason?"

"It's a long story." I thought of Jeremy. I thought of everything that led me to this point, to being here in the first place. "Not to mention, you're my boss."

"We've still got one more block. I'll drive slowly. And for the record, the boss thing—not an issue."

"Fine, let's just say I've got a past I'm not over yet."

"Mysterious . . . a recent broken leg, a need to get away, and not wanting to date anyone. Someday, you'll have to tell me the whole story."

"Someday . . ." I looked out the window, trying to avoid his gaze.

He stopped in front of my darkened house and shut off the engine.

The finality of the silence without the rumble of the engine and distant hum of the music to distract me fueled my wandering thoughts. Would he get out? Would he walk me to my door? What did I even call him?

"Um . . . should I call you Jack or J.R.?" The thought burst from my lips before I could figure out if it was even a good idea to ask.

He chuckled. "You can call me whatever you'd like. But let's just not spread it around who J.R. really is."

"Got it. Thanks for the ride."

"Not a problem." He opened his door.

I stepped out, turned, and he was already waiting there. "Whoa. You moved fast. What are you doing?"

"Walking you to your door." His eyebrows raised. "Is that okay?"

"Oh. Yeah. Of course."

He shut the passenger door for me, and I heard the beep of his horn. He followed me up the stairs leading to the door. The warmth of his body blocked the cold wind momentarily, and I shivered. My heart picked up speed, feeling him so close behind me. I used my keys to unlock the door and tried to keep my thoughts focused on the task at hand: Getting inside without doing something stupid.

"Do you have jumper cables?"

"Uh. I think I might somewhere. I'll have to look."

The polite, always proper girl I tended to be wanted to invite him in, like I was sure my mother would have, or at least I thought she might—I couldn't actually remember if that was something she would do. And then there was the other part of me, the part that suddenly couldn't stop wondering what it would be like to just let go. Forget for a while that I was some damaged girl who carried too many complications with her, and just invite him in. Throw caution to the wind, forget he was my boss, and just live.

"Do you want to come in?" I found myself saying. A knot formed my throat at my mouth's betrayal.

He gave a half-smile. "No. I should get home. It's late, but I *will* take you up on that some other time."

"Okay."

The heat of his body so close to mine sent goose bumps down my arms and legs. My resolve to keep this professional weakened just a little bit more.

"What time should I come back in the morning?"

"I can be ready anytime, just tell me when to be ready. You're doing me a huge favor."

He pulled his phone from his pocket and held it out to me.

I shot him a questioning glance.

"Your number?"

I reached to take it, and my fingers brushed his as he pulled his hand away. He quickly shoved his hand back into his pocket.

"Guess you didn't need fate after all." I pursed my lips at his smiling face.

"I don't know. This kind of feels like fate."

My hand shook as I dialed my own number and followed the steps to add it to his contacts. With the press of a button, his screen went dark again.

"I'll probably be headed to the office around eight-thirty. It's kind of early, but I've got a conference call at nine o'clock I can't get out of. Is that okay?"

"Are you kidding? You're doing me a favor. I'll be ready when you need me to be."

"I'll call you when I'm headed over. Is that enough notice?"

"Yeah."

My hand settled into the palm of his, the hard plastic and glass the only things separating our skin. I took a compulsory step forward. My hand shifted, causing the phone to drop, and it tumbled to the ground.

"I'm sorry!" I bent quickly to retrieve it. I clutched it tight in my hand and stood up so fast, my head collided with his.

"Ow," we said in unison.

He was still slightly bent over.

"I'm so sorry!"

He chuckled, rubbing his forehead while the back of my head ached. "Don't worry about it."

I pressed the phone into his hand and looked up to him to make sure he had it.

My eyes closed, cursing myself for being so klutzy.

The warmth of his breath tickled my skin, sending desire through me. The burning hunger to close the distance between us and press my lips to his filled me with such an urgency. The fear that I couldn't stop myself plagued my mind, and I stumbled backwards like I'd touched something hot.

"Whoa." Jack grabbed my arm to keep me from falling. "You okay?"

I nodded fast. "Oh yeah, I'm fine." *Just a bumbling fool, that's all.*

His face registered confusion, but only for a fleeting moment. "I should go." He looked towards his car. "See you in the morning?"

I nodded, and he strode away.

I let my head fall back against the door and closed my eyes.

*What the heck was that?*

My hands still shook, long after I'd heard his car pull away. I chugged a glass of water, hoping it would help my restless body. Marching upstairs to bed, I hoped my mind would settle long enough to allow sleep to take me away from this mess.

# Chapter EIGHT

**SUNLIGHT STREAMED THROUGH** my bedroom window, waking me far sooner than I would have liked. Yawning, I rolled over, trying to block it out, when the memory of the night before came back to me. I thought about the time Jack and I spent together over the weekend. Being here had given me peace, but being with him had given me fun in that peace. Something I hadn't known I was missing, and now it was all I could think about.

I rolled out of bed, knowing I wasn't going to fall back to sleep now, and I needed to search for the jumper cables anyway.

I threw on my slippers and trudged down to the garage, the only place I had boxes left, and there weren't many.

One glance into the first one, and I knew the cables weren't there. It was filled with clothes I'd brought for winter; a huge puffy jacket, in particular. The next box was all kinds of random things I didn't even know why I'd packed. A couple photo albums I didn't remember anything from, some cords I wasn't sure what they went to and couldn't leave them behind, just in case, and a bunch of pens and pencils, but no jumper cables.

*Great.*

I'd hoped to be less of an inconvenience, yet now I didn't have a way to get the car started. I'd have to find another way. There had to be someone else I could call for this.

*Think, Melanie.*

A tow truck? They could do that type of thing, right? I'd have to call for one once I got to work.

My phone rang. I could hear it from in the garage. I dashed into the house, leaving the boxes open where they lay. I reached it just as the ringing stopped. The number was unfamiliar, but I figured it was Jack.

I called back right away, and he picked up on the first ring.

"Hello?"

"Hey, it's Melanie. Sorry, I was in the garage."

"Oh, good. I thought I might have woken you."

"Nope."

"I'm headed that way. Are you ready?"

"I'll make sure I am."

"See you in a few."

With that, I heard a click on the line and rushed upstairs.

Fifteen minutes later, the doorbell rang just as I was putting on the last bit of lip gloss.

I slipped on my shoes and ran down the stairs, stumbling briefly when my feet hit the landing.

"Oomph."

I yanked open the door. "Hey."

"Good morning," he said.

"Come in. Let me grab my purse." I darted for the living room, where I'd tossed it from the stairs the night before. A few things had spilled out on the floor. I dropped to my knee and scooped it all up in one swift move.

Jack's footsteps echoed behind me on the wood floor. "This place is really nice."

"Thanks. It's nice and small for me."

"What changes have you made?" He stepped in further, turning around to look at everything.

"Ah . . . I painted most of the downstairs. I'm still working on that. I'm refinishing the stairs too. Still have a lot of work to do on them." I looked around, ticking each of the things off on my fingers. "I haven't touched the kitchen yet. I plan to refinish the cabinets."

"Wow, it looks great. Anything upstairs?"

My eyes followed his up the staircase, and my nerves shot into my stomach just thinking of him being in my bedroom.

"Nope, nothing up there yet." I hovered in the doorway. "Should we go?"

He took one last look around and followed me out. He didn't wait for me to lock up, but by the time I got to the car, my door was open, and he was already behind the wheel.

"I picked up some jumper cables on my way over, just in case."

"Oh my gosh, you're a lifesaver. I couldn't find any this morning. I was going to call a tow truck when we got to the office."

"Oh no. I'd never let you do that."

"I'll pay you back."

"No." He waved me off. "I should have some in my car anyway."

"I probably should too." I still planned to pay him for them somehow. My problems should not be costing him money, it's bad enough they're taking up his time. Though, I had a feeling he wouldn't be willing to take my money.

He pulled in next to my car, keeping the front end as close to mine as possible.

"Keys?"

I handed them to him and let him go to work. I had no idea what I was doing, and by the way he moved between the two cars, he did. I watched him clamp the cables to each of the batteries, the muscle in his forearm bulging each time. Momentarily, all I could think of was what he'd look like with his shirt off, sweat running down over his chiseled abs as he bent over my car.

I shook myself. What was wrong with me? I was turning into Grace, man hungry.

Within minutes, my car finally turned over.

"Yes! Thank you so much."

"Don't thank me yet. We'll see if it starts later when you're ready to leave."

I didn't know what that meant, so I took his word for it and hoped it would.

He let it run for a few minutes as he disconnected the cables and closed both hoods, then he shut them off and handed me the keys.

A car pulled in beside us as I turned to head inside, the window rolled down. A middle-aged bald man sat in the driver's seat. "Jack?"

"That's me," Jack said.

The man turned to the passenger seat and lifted a bag to Jack's hand.

"Thanks, man."

"Anytime. Enjoy, sir." The man rolled up the window and drove away.

"Hungry?" Jack asked.

I nodded, remembering I'd skipped eating in my haste to get out the door.

"Good. I think I've got enough for ten." He laughed.

"Well, I hope Cindy's here, then."

"Oh, she is. Always is. Every morning at seven a.m. without fail."

I followed him inside and went to my desk, like every morning, but Jack stopped and turned to me. "What are you doing?"

"Getting to work." I lifted a couple files from the desk.

He shook his head. "Food first." He tipped his head towards his office, urging me to follow, and kept walking.

I heard him greet Cindy, and I smoothed my shirt before heading that way, grateful for her to be a buffer against my thoughts of him outside of the office.

She was seated at the desk inside his office, a folder open in front of her. She looked up at me, her face unreadable beyond surprise that was evident. I couldn't help but wonder if it was because she didn't expect me in here, or if she figured we'd arrived together.

I worried she didn't think I belonged back here with them, and if I was being honest, I probably didn't. Nothing I'd been thinking about Jack had been professional.

"Good morning," I said.

"Morning."

Jack gestured to the food. "Grab what you'd like, Melanie. Make yourself at home on the couch."

He sat down at his desk and started eating while he thumbed through a folder waiting for him. There were multiple colorful tabs that stuck out at different spots he paid closer attention to. Was that one of the things Cindy did for him?

I grabbed a breakfast burrito from the top.

Silence fell on the room while everyone ate, Jack and Cindy both engrossed in their work. It was strange being there with nothing to busy myself with outside of the food in front of me, when Jack dropped the folder back to his desk and turned to me, smiling.

His eyes never left mine as he spoke to Cindy. "How was your dinner party?"

She glanced up from what she was doing. "Oh, it was fine. My mother-in-law kept staring at my stomach though, as if I'd put on weight or something."

Jack chuckled. "Of course you haven't. Maybe she's just hoping for grandchildren."

Cindy shuddered. "That woman would drive me crazy if I were pregnant."

"Is she terribly involved?" I asked. I knew a thing or two about feeling like you were under a microscope, and I hated it.

"Yes! Most of the time, it's fine, she's sweet, but sometimes I just want some space. Goodness. I can't even imagine when we decide to have kids. She'll probably move in so she can clean my house for me, so I don't have to lift a finger."

"Well, that doesn't sound so bad," Jack said.

"The cleaning part, no. Her being there twenty-four-seven, bad. Very bad."

I pushed the last of my burrito in my mouth and stood. "I should get to work."

Jack looked as if he was going to argue, when Cindy pointed to a stack at the corner of his desk. "That one is ready for you."

I nodded, grabbing it and leaving his office without another glance in Jack's direction.

It felt good to get out of there. The electric buzz between me and Jack was stifling when Cindy sat there, never the wiser. I wondered if Jack felt it too, then I cursed myself for letting my mind go there once again.

That afternoon, I followed Cindy out.

"Thanks again for covering for me last night."

"Oh, it wasn't a problem at all."

"I just feel terrible that after covering for me, your car wouldn't start. What a day for that to happen."

"It happens. Hopefully, it'll start now."

"You aren't sure it will?" Cindy asked.

"Jack . . . err . . . J.R. said he wasn't sure it would."

"Do you want me to wait with you, in case it doesn't?"

"Oh, no." I shook my head. "Go on. I'll just call a tow truck if I need to."

"All right. See you tomorrow." She waved and got into her car.

I unlocked the door and took a deep breath. "Come on, baby, start." I turned the key.

Nothing.

I tried three more times out of desperation. Dead.

I sighed.

Locking the car, I headed back inside, where I knew Jack was still working. Dropping my purse on my desk, I pulled out my phone and called the first five-star rated tow truck service I came across.

A gruff man picked up on the third ring. "Al's towing. What can I do for ya?"

"Hi, I'm looking for someone who can tow my car to the shop."

"Do you have one already in mind?"

"Oh, uh . . . I hadn't thought that far ahead. Is it okay if I figure that out while I wait?"

"That's fine."

"Melanie?" Jack came out of his office, looking confused. "I thought you left."

"We charge fifty dollars for the first twenty miles and a dollar twenty-five per mile after," the man said in my ear.

I nodded, listening.

"What are you doing?" Jack whispered next to me. I could tell he was trying to hear what was being said.

"That sounds fine." I held a finger up to Jack and mouthed, "Tow truck."

"Alrighty then, I just need to know where I'm sending the truck, and what kind of car."

Jack snatched the phone from my hand and held it to his ear. "I'm sorry to bother you, but we won't be needing that truck after all. Have a great evening." He pressed a button to end the call and set it down on the desk.

"Why did you do that?" I protested.

"Because you don't need your car towed."

I planted my hand on my hip but immediately regretted it when a sharp pain shot through my ribcage. I leaned over and grabbed my aching side. "H-how am I going to get my car driving then?" I breathed in and out slowly.

Jack's eyes traveled to my hand and back to my eyes. "It's just a dead battery. We'll go get a new one, and it'll be just fine . . . are you all right?"

"What?" I breathed.

He pointed to my hunched over posture and my hand on my ribs.

"Oh, I'm fine, just a stitch." I stood straight, quickly biting back the ache that grew with standing. "So it's just a battery, you think?"

"I know. Probably one of the easiest fixes."

"Well, I don't know how to do that, so I still need the tow truck." I reached for my phone.

He batted it out of my hand. "Stop."

"What? I can't ask you to keep doing all these things for me. It's bad enough I took up your time last night and this morning."

"I'm glad to do it."

"You know how to change it?"

He pursed his lips.

I eyed him, considering my options. Sitting here to wait for a tow truck and dealing with a shop, or going with Jack to the store, coming back, and leaving with a running car. The latter seemed like the better option despite it being a terrible idea to spend extra time with him.

"Okay," I relented.

"Give me five minutes." He strode back into his office.

The minute he left my view, I sunk into the chair and breathed through the pain, clutching my side until finally it subsided.

It had been a while since I'd felt any pain in my ribs. They ached sometimes, but nothing like that. Something about the way I'd popped my hip out didn't sit well. I'd have to remember not to do that again. I never wanted to recreate that pain, especially like that. I almost had to tell Jack something. He was going to wonder more and more about why I had all these weird injuries.

But I wasn't ready to go there. Not with him. He didn't need to know. He's my boss, after all, no matter how much my mind thought about him as anything but. I couldn't let things go there.

Could I?

The possibility of moving on in my own way excited me, in a way I could never remember feeling. Though, I was sure at some point I had, maybe for Jeremy.

Minutes later, he made his way out, and I followed him, just like the night before.

Silence fell between us as Jack maneuvered his car onto the street. I had no idea where we were going. I couldn't even picture an auto parts store I'd seen since moving here. But it wasn't a parts store he turned into and parked. It was a tiny Italian restaurant that looked no bigger than my house.

"I thought we were getting a battery?"

"We are . . . after we eat." He shut off the car and turned towards me, smiling a huge, toothy grin.

I narrowed my eyes. "Somehow I get the feeling you planned this."

"What? How could I plan your battery going out? Nah . . . but I may have hoped." With that, he hopped out and waited at the curb for me to follow.

I couldn't stop my lips from curving upwards, though I tried my best to hide it from him.

Stepping through the door made my stomach flop, and my nerves ignited. The romantic atmosphere was made for couples.

Once we were seated and our orders taken, the silence set in, making me squirm. I didn't feel comfortable looking right at him, yet looking anywhere around the room, seeing the other couples, made my stomach flop, so I settled for staring at my water glass and the way it made the objects beyond it larger.

Then we made eye contact.

I felt it within my core, like he was looking deep into my soul. It was too much. Too soon. I blushed, pulling my eyes away again. Though now it seemed flirty, and I hated myself for it.

"Mommy's girl, or Daddy's girl?" he asked.

My brows furrowed. "What?" *What kind of question was that?*

"Growing up, were you a Mommy's girl or a Daddy's girl?"

"Ah . . ." How did one answer that without memories from their childhood? I honestly didn't have a clue. I thought of the climate in the house after my accident, the constant hovering from my mom, and then the sweet side of my dad. I'd have to guess. I mean, it didn't really matter that much, did it? "Daddy's girl." I gulped as the words came out.

Was it really a lie if you didn't know the correct answer? Probably.

"I suspected that."

"Why?"

"I don't know . . . the way you present yourself, I guess. Proud. Not willing to accept help easily."

Was he right? I thought of my actions to avoid getting closer to him, and I supposed some could be construed that way; however, maybe part of it was something else entirely. Something deep-seated inside me. Something I hadn't even realized was a driving force—the need to do things on my own. But wasn't that why I was here in the first place?

Ugh. Such a simple question, wound with so much doubt and confusion.

"It's not an insult," Jack said when I still said nothing more.

"Oh. Of course not."

He nodded. "What about your favorite food? That might be a safer topic." He grinned, showing he noticed my hesitancy.

"Mexican."

"Really? I know a really good place. It's kind of a hole-in-the-wall, but there aren't many Mexican restaurants around here, and even fewer good ones. I'll have to take you there sometime."

"I'd like that." And then I realized it sounded like I'd just agreed to a second date. I bit my cheek when my heart betrayed me and skipped a beat at the thought. *Stop* . . . "What's yours?"

"Barbecue. Basically, anything made on a grill. Steak, burgers, chicken, I love it all."

"Yum."

"I do make some mean steaks." He licked his lips.

I bit mine, watching his tongue slowly glide across his, and my breath hitched. I shook my head and shoulders, trying to snap myself out of it.

"You okay?" he asked.

"Yep . . . fine. Just got . . . a chill."

"Are you cold?" He made a move to get up. "I have a sweater in the car . . ."

"No, no. I'm fine."

He settled his napkin back in his lap as our food was placed in front of us.

"I've got one for you."

"Let's hear it." He pushed a forkful of steaming lasagna into his mouth and breathed between his teeth. "Hot."

I giggled, chirpy and high-pitched. *Where did that come from?* I was beginning to sound like a teenage girl on her first date.

"Phew, that was a lot hotter than I thought it was. Sorry, what did you want to know?"

"Where have you traveled?"

"Ever?" he asked, his eyes wide.

I nodded, leaning over to take a bite.

"And we aren't counting just passing through, right?"

I shook my head.

"Good, I doubt I could even name all those. Let's see, in the U.S., I've been to New York, Florida, Texas, Alabama, Arizona, California, Washington, oh, and Maine. There's probably some I'm forgetting." He stared at the ceiling as if he was thinking through them all.

"And you've been out of the country?" I asked.

"Mexico, Canada, and Ireland."

"Wow, you've been all over."

"My favorite was Ireland. It was so beautiful there. I can't wait to go back. Have you been?"

"Ah . . ." *No? Yes? Have I?* Where have I been? Knowing the little I did about my parents and the few pictures of us in different places, I was certain we'd traveled. But I had no clue where.

My cheeks heated as the seconds passed without an answer. His gaze fell on me, and only the sound of my uneven breathing and blood coursing through my veins filled my ears. "Will you excuse me?"

I fled so fast, I didn't even catch his response. A rush of emotion came over me. Tears burned my eyes, and I couldn't stop them, no matter how hard I tried. A couple tears escaped before I made it to the security of the bathroom. I hovered over the sink, bracing myself on the counter.

I wanted to know where I'd been. But more than anything, I wanted to feel normal again. To be able to go out on a date and be able to tell someone about myself. Except that wasn't reality for me. My memories only included the last few months, and that wasn't a lot to go on.

I wanted this with Jack. I was beginning to feel things I couldn't stop. How could I already want this hypothetical future so badly, it brought tears to my eyes?

I glared at myself in the mirror. Tear-streaked redness had already begun to fade. Who would want to get involved with this mess anyway? They'd have to be crazy.

I gave my cheeks a quick slap, reddening them to match the rest of my blotchy skin, and ventured back out into the dimly lit dining room.

"This is a really cute place."

"It is." He eyed me a little too closely for comfort. There was a flicker of something in his eyes, and then it was gone again. "The couple that own it were married here . . . shoot . . . probably around fifty years ago, when it was a reception hall. But then the place went belly-up, and they knew they had to buy it. They opened this place with the last of their money. She used all her great-grandmother's recipes from back in Italy."

"Wow, that's incredible. Do they still run it?"

He shook his head. "Their kids. Though I still see them in here every now and then."

"I hope to meet them someday."

He reached over and covered my hand with his. My breath hitched in my throat at the sensation of his skin on mine. I stared up into his eyes, and the burning heat in them made me falter, forgetting everything else for just that moment.

A crash of plates rang out through the restaurant. I yanked my hand back and looked around. It was all I needed to bring me back to my senses. Though, immediately, I wished it hadn't.

"We should go." I hopped up from the table.

Jack nodded and stood, pulling his wallet from his pocket.

I followed him through the restaurant, feeling pangs of regret that the small moment we had was over. I fought the urge to reach out and grab his hand.

While Jack paid at the counter, the waitress came over and handed him a bag. "Dessert to go."

Jack grinned at her and kissed her cheek. "You're too kind."

She smiled back, nodded to me, and was off again, taking care of another table.

"What was that about?" Jealousy spiked within me, even though I had no right to those feelings. I had no claim here. All I had was wanting and hope. Hope I could find a new job, because these feelings were running rampant, and there was no stopping them now.

"Standing order."

I looked at him.

"Come on." He waited until he was behind the wheel to finish talking. "A few years ago, around the time I moved here, I stumbled upon this place. I'd finished college, and I'd already had a lot of experience with investments and financial endeavors through my parents. Somehow, I got to talking with the owners who, at the time, were struggling to stay afloat and had been for a while. They were facing the choice to close or sell. I helped them turn it around, and ever since, they have a standing order for take-home dessert on the house."

Totally not what I expected. Words didn't come, and the car stayed quiet as he backed out of the spot.

"It's kind of crazy, really. Even the newbies who don't know me always seem to know. It's like they have a picture of me or something in the kitchen."

I laughed. "That's so funny."

"I know." He grinned. "But you'll never find a better cannoli, so I'll never complain."

Once we were back at my car, new battery in tow, Jack set straight to work. At one point, he wiped his brow with the shoulder of his Oxford shirt, and his eyes found mine. He didn't smile or even make a face. The serenity behind his eyes made me long to reach out and touch him, for him to pull me into his arms with those very able hands that worked their magic under my hood.

He stood up suddenly and pressed the hood down. The loud slam startled me.

"All done." He tossed me the keys. "Why don't you give it a try?" He held up his greasy hands for me to see.

I made a face and moved to the driver's seat.

The engine turned over the first time.

"Yes!" I spoke under my breath, shut it off, and climbed out. "What a relief. Thank you so much!"

"No problem." He turned and started walking to the building.

The urge to follow propelled my feet forward after him.

"You'll have to let me pay you for your time," I called after him.

"Not a chance." He pulled a card from his pocket, held it up to the door, and it unlocked.

He held the door open wide with just his wrist to minimize the grease transfer. The office was dark, like walking into a cave. The door shut behind us, and I made my way in the miniscule light cast out by the emergency exit signs to the light switch. I reached for the switch, but my hand found warm flesh.

Jack had beat me there. We froze, my hand resting on his arm.

His breath was on my face, and I could just make out the outline of his features that hovered above mine. My free hand came to rest on his chest, and I could feel the rise and fall as his breaths came, rough and even.

My lips parted. Without a single thought, I was kissing him. My body responded in ways I couldn't remember feeling. His lips were so soft, so inviting. My heart soared to feel him as I yearned to for weeks despite my drive to deny myself this one glorious moment.

And then my thoughts came back to me, nagging me. I pulled away, looking him in the eyes. The fear that I'd just royally screwed up filled my stomach.

My eyes fell to my hands, which were gripping his shirt, as if I might fall the second I let go.

I released him and backed away.

"I'm so . . ." I whispered.

I couldn't finish. Jack took a step forward, and his arms went around me as he pulled me against him. He pressed his lips to mine with such intensity, it took my breath away.

My arms wrapped around his neck, and I rose up on my toes to meet him. One of his hands roamed up my back and pushed into my hair, cupping the back of my head gently. He backed me up further, pressing me against my desk.

I was panting when he pulled away.

"I've been wanting to do that since I saw you in the coffeehouse," he breathed. "And to think you've been right under my nose this whole time."

I didn't know what to say. My head swam in all that was right and all that was so very wrong. We were in the office, for goodness sake. He was my boss. Not to mention he had no idea what kind of baggage I carried with me.

I searched for something to say. Anything. Yet words failed me.

He leaned down with a smirk on his face and brushed his lips against mine once more. Then he flipped on the light.

He pursed his lips. "I may have gotten a little grease on you . . ."

My eyes averted his and checked my arm where he'd gripped me.

"I'm thinking it's in other places as well . . ." His eyes flickered to my hair and then to the floor. "I should go clean up."

I watched him walk away to the bathroom, until the door shut, snapping me from my trance.

*What had I done?*

I'd just crossed the line I'd drawn, like it never existed. And now, I had no idea how to handle this. My mind spun, and my heart raced still from the spark he'd incited inside me.

I had to get out of here.

I pulled two twenties from my wallet, jotted a quick apology and thank you, and left them under a rock in front of the front door. Maybe it wasn't the best approach, but it was all I had.

I hightailed it to my car. The urge to both hide in a cave and leap for joy overwhelmed me. His touch electrified me unlike anything I could have ever imagined. So alive and guilty. Guilty like a dog sneaking food off your plate, I knew I shouldn't go there; however, the temptation had been too great. And now I was running away.

What on Earth was I going to do now? The thought of going to work tomorrow felt stifling.

As soon as I got home, paying no attention to the time, I called Grace.

Regardless of her boy-crazed antics, I knew she would be able to make me feel better and maybe even come up with some great fix to this mess that she helped create. After all, if she hadn't orchestrated our little mini date over the weekend, my feelings for him would never have been so hard to deny. I mean, his looks were amazing and enough to make any girl blush, but I'd like to think I'd have a bit more control over myself.

"What's up? You're up late. Don't working people go to bed early?" Grace's voice flooded my ear.

"Not tonight they don't, and for what it's worth, there may not be any sleep in store for me tonight."

"Whoa, what did I start? You partying without me?" I could hear her giggling in the background.

"I kissed Jack."

Her giggles stopped. "Jack, the guy I introduced you to at the club?"

"The very one. Who, by the way, also happens to be my boss."

"Wait, what? I thought Cindy was your boss?"

"Well, she's the one that hired me, and she's who I see all day while my boss has been cooped up in his office. Or not . . . turns out, he has his own private exit."

"*That* is weird."

"He didn't want people to know who he was."

"Why?"

"Same reason I made you swear not to tell anyone about my trust."

"Wait, so he's rich?"

"I guess. I mean, he owns the company I work for."

"Wow. So, back to the kiss. How was it?"

"Amazing, but that's *so* not the point."

"I knew it! And yes, it's the *only* point. If it was bad, you wouldn't be calling me."

She was right, of course. If the kiss had been terrible, that would have made all of this so much easier. I could have walked away, gone back to work like nothing happened.

"What are you saying?" I asked.

"What I'm *saying* is, the decision was already made. Are you going to be able to go back to the way things were before? Working with Cindy and pretending not to know who's behind that office door?"

"No."

"Okay, then all you have to do is decide if you can work under him or not . . . and I don't mean in the bedroom." She giggled again.

"Grace!"

"What? He's gorgeous."

"I *know.*" I bit my lip.

And I did. I knew only too well how good he looked. Those green eyes hadn't left my mind.

"So?" Grace asked.

"So, I don't know. It would be so weird. And what would Cindy think? I don't want to be that girl. Heck, I didn't even want to date in the first place. I mean, it feels like yesterday I broke up with Jeremy. How am I supposed to just cast that away like it never happened?"

"Jeremy? Psh, he's got nothing on Jack."

I shook my head. "This is exactly what I'd been hoping to avoid when I first met him."

"At the club?" Grace asked. "It's not like it's been that long . . ."

"No. I already knew him when you 'introduced' us at the club. I told you that at the time."

She was silent for a moment. "Wait, now you've lost me."

I sighed. "You were so focused on Alex to hear, I think. I met Jack the day I was called for the interview. He introduced himself at the coffeehouse."

"And?"

"And nothing. I tried to avoid him every chance I could. He even ran into me once, knocked me flat on my butt. But he kept showing up! Then you came into the picture."

"It's a good thing I did! Why would you avoid all that goodness?" she all but yelled into the phone.

"You know why. It's just too complicated with . . . with everything."

She groaned. "When are you just going to start living and put it all behind you? I thought that was the point of moving in the first place?"

"Yes and no. I don't need a date, let alone a boyfriend, in order to move on."

"Then is it even moving on? To me, it sounds like only half a life."

"But what if that's enough for me?"

"Then you're lying to yourself. I've got to go, I've got therapy in the morning, and this convo turned sad fast. I'm hoping I get a call from you very soon with really good news, that's all I'm going to say."

I rolled my eyes. "Uh huh, bye."

Ugh. For the first time, Grace had done nothing but make me feel more wound up.

I needed something to calm me. I headed for the kitchen and grabbed a mug.

Five minutes later, I breathed in the soothing aroma of my favorite cinnamon tea as I sank to the floor pillow by the window.

*I really need to get a couch.*

A soft knock sounded on the door. I stared at it for a moment, nervous about who it could be this late at night.

I set the mug down on the floor and padded to the door, hoping not to be heard, just in case I decided not to answer.

Peeking through the peephole, I saw Jack standing there, his hands in his pockets, and my stomach dropped.

Slowly, my fingers found the lock, and I pulled the door open.

"Hey," I said. "Is something wrong?"

"Can I come in?"

I looked back and forth between his eyes. The worry in them had me pushing the door open faster than I could blink.

He made his way into the living room. I followed him in but passed him to sit back where I'd been before he'd knocked. He seemed to question where to sit, and I tossed him a floor pillow.

"Haven't taken the time to buy a couch."

"I'm sorry to just drop in like this. I couldn't let things go after you ran out like that. Did I take things too far?"

Oh, man. This was happening. We were going to get real, fast. I'd hoped to avoid this at least until morning, when I'd had a little more time to process, but here it was. Standing in front of me in dress slacks and a button-down shirt.

Breathing in the steam, I took a sip of my tea.

"No. You didn't."

"Why did you run out like that?"

I focused my sight into the mug, though I still felt his eyes on me.

"Melanie." His voice was soft.

"I didn't know what to say. I tried really hard not to let things go there . . . I failed."

"Failed? That's how you see this?"

"That didn't come out right."

"Do you mean because you work for me? Because that's not an issue for—"

I put my hand up, cutting him off. "Yes, but that's not the only reason. I didn't plan to get involved with anyone, especially so soon. That's why I avoided you before . . ." I looked into his eyes, hoping he would understand.

"You were avoiding me?"

"I tried to. My curiosity about you scared me, not to mention the attraction." I blushed. "I just can't commit to a relationship right now."

"Why?"

"It's complicated."

His lips went tight. "And you aren't ready to talk about it, right?"

I didn't lift my gaze from the floor and twitched my head from side to side.

*I'm not ready for you to look at me differently. Like I'm broken.* The words screamed in my head, yet I refused to say them. Refused to let him see the me that was only half there. The guilt of not coming clean ate at me, and my stomach churned.

He reached over and grasped my hand between his fingers. "Look, I don't know what you've been through; however, I can tell by the haunted look in your eyes, it's not been easy. I know we don't know each other very well yet. I'd like to be there for you in any way you'll let me." He reached over and lifted my chin, making me look at him. "I know I'm your boss and that freaks you out, but it doesn't bother me, and I'm almost certain if Cindy knew, she'd be ecstatic. She's been trying to fix me up with someone forever."

I bit my lip.

"I'm going to leave this in your court. If you felt even half of what I did from that kiss . . ." He let that thought hang in the air. "I really would like to give this a try."

When I didn't answer, he dropped my hand and stood. His eyes were everywhere, except on me.

"I'll go. But please, think about it?"

I lifted my eyes to meet his gaze again when his voice cracked with his last words. Only for the briefest moments did he hold it, and then he strode out of my house.

My heart urged me to go after him, to do something, anything, except sit here, dumbstruck. But I didn't.

I listened to his car door close and the engine turn over, and I settled deeper into the cushion against the wall.

Putting my cup to my mouth, I didn't plan to move from this spot until I knew exactly what to do.

***

A car honking outside jolted me awake. My arm smacked into the mug, spewing the water I'd refilled it with everywhere.

"Crap."

As I lifted myself off the hardwood floor, every joint and muscle screamed in pain.

Why had I thought staying here would be the best idea?

I reached for my phone, searching for the time. It was bathing in the water.

"Double crap."

I jumped up and ran to the kitchen for a towel, saw the time on the stove, and freaked.

"I'm late!"

I threw on the first work-appropriate clothes I found and flew out the door. It wasn't until I pulled into work and saw Jack's car that the night before came back into focus. My heart sank. Even though I'd made up my mind before drifting off to sleep sometime late last night, I worried about the backlash it could have. Though, hope and excitement for what could be had wound itself around all that worry, creating a knot of emotion as big as a boulder in the pit of my stomach.

What would Cindy think? Would we even tell her?

But when I made my way inside, it was like nothing had changed. Though, I don't know what I expected. A stack of files waited for me, just like every other morning. Cindy and Jack were more than likely holed away in his office, working.

By lunchtime, I was beginning to wonder if I'd even see anyone today. Cindy hadn't emerged from the office once, and I'd finished all my work long before. The book I'd kept in my purse for times like now kept my mind from spinning on what Jack was thinking.

Had he changed his mind? Was he avoiding me? Or was he just working like normal? *This was why office romances didn't work*, I chastised myself.

I'd lost myself in the book when Jack cleared his throat beside me, making me jump out of my skin.

"H-hey." I stood quickly, dropping my book on the desk.

"Hey, I'm sorry I haven't made it out until now. I've been on conference calls all morning, and Cindy called in sick. Couldn't have possibly been a worse day for it. I've been scrambling." He rubbed his forehead and blew out a breath. "It's just been one thing after another. Do you want to grab some lunch? I really need to get out of this office."

His green eyes sparkled down at me, and if by nothing more than magical force, I rose up on my toes and pressed my lips to his. It was gentle at first, and then Jack's arms pulled me in. His lips were as warm and inviting as his arms. I settled into him, deepening the kiss. A soft moan escaped and muffled against his lips.

He pulled back with a grin that spread all the way to his eyes. "Please tell me that means you've decided to give us a go."

A simple nod was all it took for him to lift me into his arms and plant another quick kiss on my lips.

"You have no idea how happy that makes me."

*** 

It was two days before Cindy came back to work, and for those couple days working together, just the two of us, it was like living in a little blissful bubble. In the back of my mind, I couldn't stop the worry of what Cindy would think when she came back, even though I didn't know when that would be.

I'd come to enjoy working with Jack, and what seemed to be our new routine. He always stopped by the coffeehouse to pick up coffee on the way, so I couldn't complain. I took a sip just as Cindy walked in. The vulnerability of being the first one to see her, the guilt weighed me down like concrete. My mind spun, thinking she surely must know something. Darn Jack for hiding out in his office, leaving me to face her alone.

"Good morning, Melanie."

"Morning."

"Thanks for holding down the fort while I was sick. Worst flu of my life! Couldn't keep anything down."

"Oh, bummer. Glad you're feeling better."

"Me too."

Then she made her way into his office, just like every other day, and I felt ridiculous. Surely, she wouldn't know anything just by looking at me. I shook my head. *You're so dumb.*

However, with her being in his office, he would tell her. Wouldn't he?

I bit my nail. How soon would he tell her? I was on edge all day, wondering at what point she would come out knowing.

At lunchtime, Jack ordered lunch to be delivered. Pasta. Except when it arrived, he hooked his finger to me, inviting me into his office. It was something we'd done every day while Cindy was gone. Now that she was back, I hadn't expected it to continue.

Cindy smiled at me as I settled myself on his couch, full plate in hand. It was when Jack came over and sat beside me that her eyebrows lifted and her expression changed. Guiltily, I looked at my plate.

"What's this?" she asked.

"Cindy, I'd like you to meet my new girlfriend." The smiled that encompassed Jack's face as he stared down at me made my stomach flop.

"When did this happen?"

"Two days ago," he said.

"Wow. I knew there was something different about you this morning, Jack. You were too . . . happy."

"Sheesh. You make me sound like a grump!"

"You are a grump! But I'm happy for you guys. I guess this means she'll be coming to the barbecue this weekend?"

He turned to me. "The barbecue. I almost forgot about that. Yes. I certainly hope so."

# Chapter NINE

**I HELD THE** glass casserole dish filled with cheesy potatoes between my hip and arm as I gawked at Jack's house, far larger and rustic than I expected. It sat between huge pines and was surrounded by forest in every direction. His closest neighbor was probably a quarter-mile away. The views from the second-story windows must be stunning. I envisioned the trees capped with snow come winter and couldn't wait to see the beauty.

Then I realized what that meant. I was already planning my future to be with this man. And for the first time in a long time, it didn't scare me. Though, knowing I still had a big part of me even I didn't know made me question whether he would still see that future if he knew.

I could hear voices coming from the back yard and spotted the open gate. Jack had been vague about who would be here today, but I figured I'd be meeting his friends. The butterflies, the friends I never leave home without lately, had made their presence known once again in the pit of my stomach.

His back yard was nothing like I would have expected. One long table lined with a crisp white table cloth, with assorted river rocks in the center, surrounding white candles. Way more elegant than the normal barbecue I thought I'd be going to, and nothing like I would have expected from Jack.

Jack stood on the deck next to the grill. I giggled seeing him in an apron. It took only a few moments for him to spot me. He waved me over as he lifted the lid of the grill and checked on the chicken.

There were so many people, only two of which I knew. I made my way quickly over to Jack, setting the casserole down at the food table on the way. I was just steps away when a tall blonde stepped in my way.

"*Who* are you?" she demanded.

"I, uh . . ." I tried to look around her to catch Jack's eye, but he was focused on the grill.

"*Hello?*" She bent down, putting her face in front of mine.

"M-melanie." The stutter in my voice made me wince. Why couldn't I be more like Grace? So in your face, without a care what you think.

"Well, I'm sorry, *Melanie,* this is my party. I think you might be lost."

I had no idea who this woman was, but I didn't have a single nice feeling towards her. Though, deep inside me, I had an innate drive to be polite. After all, I was at Jack's house, for the first time.

"I'm not lost. I'm here with Jack."

At this, the woman burst out laughing, turning back towards Jack. "Jack," she said through her laughter. "This girl says she's here with you. Isn't that just the funniest thing you've ever heard?"

Her loud voice carried over everyone else at the party. I froze, feeling every single eye land on me, their conversations stalled. Jack stepped around the rude woman in front of me and put his arm around me.

"Oh good, I see you've met Melanie. Everyone, this is my girlfriend." He kissed me quickly on the cheek before he pulled me over to the grill.

My nerves were still rattling. He grasped both my hands in his and gave me a long, tender kiss that had me melting. Every nerve relaxed.

"Ignore my sister," he whispered. "Her name's Bianca. I don't think she took the time to introduce herself. She's getting married in a few months. She's been a bit of a bridezilla lately, and, well, I don't bring girls home, so I think you were a bit of a shock."

I couldn't decide if I should be upset he didn't tell me he never brought girls to meet his family or inform me I'd be meeting his family in the first place.

I turned back to look at the tall blonde again. His sister. I'd never been more grateful to have that inner voice telling me to be polite. I really would have made a fool of myself if I'd have told her off. Phew.

Now that I looked more closely at her, I could see some resemblance. She had Jack's green eyes and that same sneaky grin. Other than that, she was all her own.

From the moment I stepped next to Jack, a steady flow of people came to meet me. It was clear I was meeting just about everybody who was important in Jack's life, and many who weren't and were only there with the groom. Though, from what I'd managed to gather, the groom and bride's families had known each other for a long time.

Then, just as I thought I'd met everyone, an older couple stepped up in front of us. From the loving yet inquisitive look on the woman's face, I guessed she could only be one person.

"Hello," she said, looking from me to Jack. "I'm Ruth, Jack's mother."

"Hi," I said quickly.

"James, the dad." He winked and extended his hand, which I took.

"This is Melanie," Jack said, introducing me. "My girlfriend."

Warmth crept to my cheeks. I'd forgotten to tell them my name. I smiled sheepishly at them.

His mom leaned in and embraced me, very lightly. "I'm so glad to meet you."

Jack interrupted my response, announcing the food was ready. His mom and dad nodded to me and headed to the table.

When everyone had taken their seats, he pulled all the chicken from the grill, and I took the opportunity to ask him what I'd been wondering since I walked in.

"What is this barbecue for?" It was something I probably should have asked before, but I'd assumed it was just for fun.

"It's sort of an engagement party," he whispered. "It's a little late in the game though. It took some time to plan for when they would both be in the country."

I nodded.

"Help me bring the food to the table?"

"Sure."

The last two chairs at the table were meant for us, and I made sure to grab the one next to Cindy.

"How you holding up?" she asked.

"So. Many. People," I whispered.

She snickered behind her napkin. "Most of them are really nice."

"And Bianca?"

"Eh." She shrugged. "She's not bad, just a little spoiled. Comes with the territory."

As the evening went on and the sun dipped behind the trees, twinkling lights strung above grew brighter, lighting up the back yard in the most romantic way.

As soon as dessert had been finished, guests started trickling out, saying their goodbyes and thank yous to Jack, Bianca, and her fiancé—

who I now knew as Kurt—then slipped out the gate until it was only Jack, Bianca, Kurt, me, and his parents. They gathered on the porch, and the idea of joining them made me feel like an intruder, so I made myself busy cleaning up the table instead. I kept my ears open, trying to hear what they might be saying, though their hushed tones made it impossible to hear anything. Their eyes kept flashing to me.

Eventually, Jack's mom came over, leaving the rest to talk.

"You don't have to do that, you know."

"Oh, I don't mind."

She nodded, then collected a few plates and made a neat pile.

"I think we were all a bit surprised Jack invited you today. He's never brought anyone to meet us before."

"I heard that. He didn't mention I'd be meeting all of you today."

She giggled. "Well, that does sound like my son. I guess this was a lot for all of us."

I smiled.

"I realize Bianca wasn't very welcoming earlier." She leaned forward. "It wasn't her finest moment. Something she probably feels very bad about. We would like to get to know you better, if that's okay with you."

"I'd like that."

"Great. I'll set something up. It really was good to meet you, Melanie." She lifted a stack of plates and brought them inside. Jack's dad, Kurt, and Bianca followed her inside, but not before calling out goodbye to me.

I waved and continued cleaning up the table.

Jack came up behind me and put his arms around my waist. He buried his face in my hair. "You don't have to do that."

"I know." I leaned into him. "Your mom said the same thing," I teased.

"Dance with me."

"What? There's no music."

He let go of me with one hand and did something on his phone, then music surrounded us.

I looked around, unable to hide my surprise. "Where is that coming from?"

"Speakers."

I rolled my eyes.

He spun me around and pulled me in. His chuckle vibrated against my chest. He twirled me around the back yard a few times under the beautiful night sky and twinkle lights.

"I'm not sure your family liked me."

"Are you kidding? They didn't even have a chance to get to know you, but they're intrigued, that's for sure. I don't think I've ever gotten that big of a third degree, not even when I threw a baseball through the kitchen window when I was eleven."

"Really?"

"Really. Trust me, they're going to love you."

"Okay."

"Did you get a chance to see the inside yet?"

I shook my head.

"Come on. I'll give you the tour."

***

A week later, I stood in front of the mirror, looking over my dress. I couldn't decide if it was the best one, but I stuck with it. I sighed and put in my silver heart earrings.

When his mother had told me she would "set something up," I hadn't realized how soon that would be. I supposed it was probably a good thing to get to know them now—if they didn't approve, things with Jack and I may not be able to get off the ground anyway.

I heard Jack's subtle knock as I slipped on my shoes.

"How do I look?"

"Well, hello to you too," he said, leaning in to kiss my cheek.

I stepped back, ignoring his hello, and held out my arms.

"You look great."

"It's not too revealing, or too . . . anything?"

He stepped inside and grabbed both my hands. "You look amazing. Breathe." He took a deep breath, wanting me to mimic.

I let it out.

"Just wait and see, my family is going to love you."

Mimosas and quiche were laid out on the table when we arrived. The waiter came over as soon as we were seated, eager to please.

"What would you like to drink?" he asked both me and Jack.

"Orange juice," we said in unison.

The whole table turned towards us, and I grinned sheepishly.

"Right away." With his unamused expression, he turned and left.

"I'm so glad you could join us this morning, Melanie."

"Me too, thanks for the invitation."

Bianca eyed me. I sipped my water, hoping to avoid her curious eye. I couldn't get a good read on her whether she was happy to see me or not.

"What is it you do for a living, Melanie?" James asked.

"Oh, um, I work in the office with Jack."

Bianca's eyebrows had never been higher. Clearly, she didn't approve of that.

"Oh? Is that where you met?" Ruth asked.

Jack shook his head. "We met at the coffeehouse, and then she tried to avoid me." He chuckled.

My mouth dropped, and my cheeks burned. His family would surely hate that.

"What? I . . ."

He slung his arm around me. "It's funny," he said, only to me, before addressing the rest of the table. "Then her friend came into town. Turns out, she was adamant about setting Melanie up with someone."

I rolled my eyes. "Much to my objection."

Jack laughed even harder. "I think Melanie about died when Grace returned with me and Alex."

"Grace didn't notice at all, with how hung up on Alex she was."

"Alex Brantley?" Bianca asked.

Jack nodded.

"Well, I could see why. He's quite the charmer."

"Anyway, we really hit it off that night. Of course, Monday afternoon at work, it was quite the surprise when I found her sitting at the reception desk, working."

"Wait, she worked for you before?" Kurt asked.

Jack nodded, an ear-to-ear grin on his face. "For almost a month. Boy, was she mad. She thought I'd planned it, like I'd known the whole time."

"You and that stupid 'no one knows who you are' rule," Bianca said with disdain.

"Hey! It's not stupid."

"It certainly is. You have money. Get over it." Bianca rolled her eyes.

"Don't start, you two," his mother interjected.

"After that, it took some convincing, but she finally relented." Jack kissed my hand.

"Well, that's quite a story," his father said.

His mother sipped her mimosa. "It certainly is."

"Where are you from, Melanie?" Kurt asked.

"Texas."

"Oh yuck, I went there once, and the bugs . . . well, let's just say I won't be in a hurry to go back again." Bianca cringed.

I laughed. "I guess I was used to them."

"Have you had the chance to meet her parents yet?" his mother asked.

"Nope. Maybe we can plan a trip to see them sometime soon." Jack turned to me, a questioning look on his face.

I gulped but quickly put a smile on my lips, nodding. This was moving fast. Too fast. Bringing home a man I'd been dating, to parents I didn't remember, sounded like the worst idea ever. Of course, Jack didn't know that, because I hadn't been brave enough to tell him.

Soon. I'd tell him soon. The right time hadn't come yet. I'd know it when it came.

"Do you have any hobbies, Melanie?" His father's eyes caught mine.

"Dad's always interested in hobbies, always wanting to know what's out there," Jack whispered in my ear.

"Not really, but I did do some facelifts on my house. Painting and sanding, that type of thing."

"Wow, I'm impressed." James nodded, his eyebrows raised.

"Me too," Jack agreed. "Dad used to make clocks in his spare time, but he hasn't for a while. Woodworking used to be one of his hobbies."

"Yes, a good clock build really relaxed me. I really should start building again."

"Anything but clocks," his mom said.

Bianca and Jack started laughing.

"Dad made a few too many clocks back in the day." Bianca looked pointedly at her mom.

"A few? *Ugh,* I can still hear them ticking and chiming. It was awful, all of them going off at once. I could hardly hear myself think." Ruth shuddered.

"Yes, well, if I recall, we made a bit of money on all those clocks. Didn't we?"

"We sure did." She lovingly looked at her husband and kissed his cheek. "Are you in school, dear?" his mother asked, turning her attention back to me.

"Uh, no. I'm considering it. I was supposed to go . . ." Suddenly, it was hard to breathe. I already was teetering on the edge of things I didn't want to share. I cleared my throat. "In August, but I'm considering a change in major, so I waited."

"Smart choice," James said. "No sense in wasting money on schooling you don't need."

"Exactly." I nodded, hoping they wouldn't push for which majors.

Just then, the waiter came by to check on the table, and I breathed a sigh of relief. He left the check with James and scurried off again in search of another table to help. Napkins landed on empty plates, and I knew things were wrapping up.

"Jack, you must bring Melanie to the Halloween party. I do apologize for the late notice; I'd have made sure to send an invite if I'd have known." Ruth smiled.

"That's a great idea, Mom," Jack agreed, then looked at me, smiling. I tried to read what it meant, but I couldn't.

Bianca stood, followed quickly by Kurt, as if they were in sync, or rather, he just followed her lead. "We should be going. Lots to be done for the wedding still."

I watched her say goodbye to her parents, then she made her way to me, leaning down to hug me.

"I'm so glad we got to have brunch. It was great getting to know you."

"You too," I managed to spit out. She still made me crazy nervous, and I couldn't figure out why.

She kissed Jack's cheek, Kurt gave a last nod, and they were gone.

"We should be going as well," Jack said.

And I, like Kurt, followed his lead and said goodbye.

Jack took my hand as we made our way to his car. My nerves were still buzzing. Everything seemed to have gone well. I really liked them, even Bianca, though I couldn't tell if that was mutual.

"I told you they would like you."

"And what makes you so sure they do?" I asked.

"My mother would never have invited you to their Halloween soiree if she didn't like you."

"Well, that's just your mom."

"She is the one to crack. If she likes you, everyone else will too."

I stuck my tongue out at him. "Well, what am I supposed to wear to this shindig? Costumes optional?"

"Oh no, you have to dress up. Everyone goes all-out. It's a pretty big deal. It's just one of the many parties my mom loves to throw, but this one, it's her favorite."

Great. Last-minute costumes usually were the worst ones, the leftovers nobody wanted. The last thing I needed was to show up with a terrible costume.

"I'll take care of the costumes, okay?" He winked. "I have a guy."

I nodded, feeling relieved. And then a thought struck me. "Wait, you aren't going to make me dress up as a clown or something embarrassing, are you?"

"You think I would do that to you?" His grin made him look incredibly guilty.

"I don't know . . ." I eyed him.

"I guess you'll just have to trust me."

***

Two days later, when a stylist showed up at my door three hours before the party, I didn't know what to expect. Jack was keeping our costumes under wraps until the very last minute. I let the woman get to work on me without a single objection.

For two hours, the woman blow-dried and curled my hair, then painted one thing after another on my face. She put one last coat on my lips and stood back, inspecting her work, before nodding and turning me around to face the mirror.

It was like she'd unlocked a beauty I didn't know I held. My face was the epitome of perfection—not a single flaw showed through, including the nice pimple that decided to show up. She'd craftily hidden it behind a carefully calculated swoop of my hair.

"Wow."

"I'll say."

I whirled around to find Jack standing in the doorway behind me. He was dressed in what I could only describe as some type of Renaissance suit. He looked enchantingly handsome. In that moment, it seemed surreal he was *my* boyfriend.

My mouth hung open for a full five seconds before I clamped it shut. I hoped Jack hadn't noticed, but when my eyes found his, the amusement there told me he had.

"You look stunning."

"I'm wearing a bathrobe. You . . ."

He put his finger up to stop me. "I'm not looking at anything but your face anyway. Amelia, you've captured the look to a T. Thank you."

"Not a problem," she said. "I'll get out of your way." She slipped out of the room, carrying her bag of all things pretty.

"Seriously though, Mel, you look amazing."

"All at your hand, but thank you."

"No, even without this." He gestured to my updo. "You always take my breath away."

My cheeks warmed, and the subtle sting of tears plagued my eyes. I pushed out a breath. *I am not going to cry.*

"So, am I wearing this bathrobe to the party? I'll look quite the spectacle, standing next to you in this." I eyed the garment bag he held.

"I don't know." He tossed the bag on my bed. "I kind of like it." He pulled me into his arms and bent to kiss me.

Normally, I would have lifted my head and welcomed his kiss with everything in me. But not right now. Not after primping for the last couple hours. We had a party to get to. A big one. One in which I had to look every bit as polished as I did right at this very moment.

I pressed my hand to his lips and giggled. "Not right now, Mister. There's nothing that's going to mess *all* this up right now." I circled my hand in front of my face.

"Okay, okay." He held his hands up in the air. "Slip into that and meet me downstairs." He winked and shut the door.

I was giddy as I headed over to open the puffy bag, anxious to see what he'd picked to match this primp session. When the zipper came down, the gown inside took my breath away. Every bit of Renaissance to match him in a perfectly crafted dark, royal blue Victorian dress that, if I didn't know any better, I'd think it was from that time. He'd done a spectacular job. Way better than I could have ever dreamed our costumes to be.

I couldn't wait to put it on. Carefully, I stepped into it, making sure to get my feet all the way through the large amount of pillowy fabric. The wide, lacy sleeves slid up over my arms, like it was made just for me. I pulled the rest of it up around my shoulders and quickly realized I needed Jack to lace me up in the back. As I stepped out of my room and peered down at the man who made me happier than I could ever remember being, my heart skipped a beat. He looked more handsome than I'd ever seen him.

"Can you . . ." As he spun around, his eyes widened and his mouth hung loosely open. I froze, looking at the adoration in his face. Nothing could ever make me feel prettier than that look right there. "I can't lace up the back."

He mounted the stairs, his eyes never leaving me. This time, I couldn't push him away. This time, I wanted nothing more than for him to press his lips to mine. The eagerness that filled me was unlike any before. Longing for nothing more than the connection I felt when he held me, when he showed his love without a single word.

He pulled away, breathless, spinning me around all in one swift move. He kissed my neck once and started lacing me up. I reached up and tapped my neck.

"What?" His husky voice filled my ear.

I tapped again in a different spot. His fingers continued working, but his mouth came closer. His breath tickled, and it sent a thrill throughout my whole body. He grazed his lips ever so lightly across my skin and pulled away.

"All done," he whispered. "We should go."

That was the last thing I wanted to do. But grudgingly, I followed him downstairs, my phone clutched in my hand. That's when I realized I didn't have a clutch to match this. Nothing I owned said Renaissance.

"Jack?"

"Hm?" he asked from the doorway.

"Would you mind carrying my phone tonight? I don't have anything that matches . . ."

He held out his hand without saying a word. He gripped my hand, the phone in-between, and led me out of my house.

The nervous jitters grew the closer we came, then the car swung into one of the ritziest neighborhoods I'd ever been in, and they surged higher. These houses were enormous, far larger than I would have guessed. My parents' huge house could probably fit inside just one of them at least five times.

"You grew up here?" I asked.

"Yep."

"These houses . . . they're incredible."

"Yeah, if you like houses bigger than you can ever clean in a week!"

I giggled.

"You think I'm kidding."

"Oh no, I know you're serious."

He turned into a circular drive already filled with cars—more cars than I would have imagined would fit in front of one of these monstrosities. Then I looked up at Jack's childhood home. Spiderwebs, gravestones, and fog gave way to the spookiest mansion on the block. I had to give his mom credit, I never would have pegged her for the spooky type.

"Wow, she did a great job decorating!"

Jack snorted. "She didn't lift a finger doing any of this. Except, of course, if you count directing all the workers on what to do and where she wanted it."

"Oh."

"Ready?" he asked.

"I think so."

I followed him through the front door, where the sounds of loud, spooky music met us. There were people everywhere. Fog hung at our feet, and cauldrons emanated more.

"Jack!" His mother seemed to come out of nowhere.

"Hi, Mom," he said, leaning down to hug her.

"Look at you guys." She cocked her head to the side. "Cutest couple costumes I've seen yet. Hello again, Melanie, I'm so glad you could come." She leaned in and gave me a quick squeeze. "Make yourself at home." She winked and was off again.

A man in a monkey suit, literally, walked by with glasses of champagne. Jack snagged two of them and handed one off to me. He pushed out his elbow, inviting me to grab on, and off we went.

Jack knew everyone, which wasn't surprising, but the way he interacted with them all showed just how in tune he was with everyone around him. Like he kept up with all their lives, yet I had no idea he had so many in his circle.

By the tenth person he introduced me to—whose name I couldn't remember, even as soon as he'd said it—I excused myself to the bathroom, leading me to a whole new predicament. Finding it.

Getting around all the people was harder than I thought it would be with this huge dress, and I didn't even want to think about going once I got there, but nevertheless, my bladder was calling.

As I rounded the corner, Bianca did too.

"Oh, sorry," I said, stopping just before I stepped on her perfect red heels.

"Melanie."

"Hi." I fidgeted with my dress sleeves. "You look great."

And she did. The bright red devil's costume, which essentially was a floor-length, tight-fitting red dress, and devil horns screamed Bianca with every fiber. Sexy in all the ways I wouldn't even begin to try to be, without even trying.

"You look . . . endearing," she said. "Where's my brother? I assume you're matching?"

"He's in there." I pointed. "We are matching. Jack picked them out."

"He did?"

I nodded.

A smirk rose on her face. "How very romantic of him. I didn't think that was in his blood. Guess that's where you come in." She winked. "I'm going to go find him."

"Okay . . ." I said, but she was already well on her way. I went back to my mission: Finding the bathroom. Then I saw the line. Where there was a line at a party, there was sure to be a bathroom at the front of it. And of course, it was right in the walkway where my dress got in the way of everyone walking by. Tugging, pulling, and smashing it down only got it so small.

A girl, who didn't look much older than me, dressed in a fringed flapper costume, stood in front of me and took notice of my struggle. She giggled to herself. I looked up to her, meeting her eyes. Though I couldn't be certain what my face might have said, I must not have looked happy.

"Oh, I'm sorry. That gown is gorgeous . . . but what a pain in the neck."

I couldn't help laughing. "It sure is, I hadn't had an issue until now. I can't even imagine how I'm going to . . ." I blushed. "Well, I guess that's probably too much information."

She leaned over, the smile never leaving her face. "If you can manage it, the trick is to hold up the whole dress and face the toilet. Less touches the grossness that way." She leaned away again.

My eyebrows raised. Why hadn't I even thought of that? My hopes began to soar. She was the first person at this party I didn't feel out of place talking to.

She held out her hand. "I'm Jaime."

"Melanie."

"This your first time at one of the Bridges' parties?"

"Yeah, that obvious?"

"Only because I've never seen you before. How do you know them?" she asked.

Another person walked by, and I pulled my dress again, trying to keep it out of the way. "Uh . . . I'm Jack's girlfriend."

I glanced up to see her mouth hanging open.

"What?" I asked, quickly worried something was wrong with my dress.

"No. Nothing. I'm sorry. I just . . . wow."

I stopped fidgeting with my dress and looked up. The confusion must have been written all over my face, so she continued.

"I'm sorry." She paused. "I grew up with Jack and Bianca. I'm just surprised, that's all. I think this is the first time Jack has ever brought a date to one of these. I mean, except for me."

She dated Jack? I knew he dated very little, but that was all I knew. We both seemed to prefer to leave the past behind us. I guess mine was more so because I didn't know much about it, so I chose not to bring it up. But now that I stared at this beautiful woman standing in front of me, a woman I just admitted not knowing how to pee with this dress to—*geez, why had I done that?*—I wanted to know more.

"Oh, don't worry, it was such a long time ago. We were teenagers. We learned fairly quickly we're so much better as friends."

What did one say to that? Preferably something. Anything. But still, I stood there with a dumbfounded look on my face.

The bathroom door opened, and Jaime turned away to step inside. Thank God.

I took the moment to dab the sweat from my forehead and take a few deep breaths so when the door opened, I'd be ready to face her. Even if only for the second before I went inside.

Light flooded out a couple minutes later, and she held the door for me, smiling just the way she had when I first laid eyes on her. She wasn't holding anything against me, so why was I acting so weird?

"Thanks." I stepped inside and shut the door.

Well, that wasn't all I should have said, but I could think of nothing more. So much for having someone to chat with.

I pulled my dress back through the door and looked up to find Jack standing nearby, talking to none other than Jaime.

I felt a twinge of jealousy as she laughed at something he'd said, pressing her hand onto his forearm, lingering longer than it should have for a friend, until his eyes fell on me. His face lit up, and he stepped around her to take my hand.

"Have you met my girlfriend, Melanie?" he asked Jaime.

"I did, while we were waiting for the restroom. I'm afraid I might have scared her a bit. I let it slip we dated ages ago."

He chuckled. "Back when the idea of a boyfriend or girlfriend alone would make you feel better about yourself."

She laughed. "Exactly."

Jack put his arm around my shoulders and gave me a small squeeze against his warm body.

"How long have you two been together?" Jaime asked.

"A couple of weeks?" Jack turned to me, questioning.

I shrugged.

Jaime's eyebrows raised. "That is hardly any time at all." Her eyes flashed between me and him. "What changed about you being so dead set against anyone coming to meet your family?"

"Everything." Jack smiled at me. "If you'll excuse us, Jaime, there's someone else I'd like to introduce Melanie to." He gave her a quick hug and kiss on her cheek, then grabbed my hand, pulling me along behind him.

He walked me to the back yard and turned, only walking just enough to be out of sight. He gently pushed my back against the wall and leaned down to kiss me. The stone wall was cold against my back and bare shoulders, but his lips were enough to send a fire coursing through my body, making me forget all about it. He didn't hold back, like he'd been waiting for this very moment for weeks. When he pulled away, we were both breathless. He rested his forehead on my shoulder while he caught his breath.

"What was that for?" I whispered.

He pressed his forehead against mine. "I've been dying to do that since I saw you earlier. Someone stopped me." He made a thinking face. "You've met almost everyone, so I figured it didn't matter much if your lips were a little less . . . colored."

He gave me a quick peck and pulled me away from the wall, guiding me to the railing overlooking the back yard. If you could even call it that. It was so enormous, I wasn't sure if there was a different name for it. The grass stretched out behind the massive mansion, though of course, there were also flowers lining the walkways, and a pool probably the size of my whole house, if you laid it all out on one single level. All of it was lit up in just the right way, and I knew it had probably taken a meticulous amount of work to get it just the way it was. Perfect.

"This place is really something," I said.

"I guess you could say that."

"You don't think so?" I asked.

He shook his head. "Don't get me wrong, I loved growing up here. There was so much to explore in the back yard, but it's just too much. Too flashy. I'd much prefer my place. It's still fairly big and still has the element of exploration in my back yard, but I don't look like I'm trying to show the neighborhood how many zeros are in my bank account."

I nodded. I completely got what he was saying. It was the very thing I wondered about my parents. Why they felt the need to have a fancy house and fancy cars. Though, theirs was nowhere near this. This was an entirely different story. And from this view, my parents looked very normal.

We stood there for a moment, staring down at it all. Jaime still nagged at the back of my mind. Did she gallop around through the grass with him when they were kids? Probably. And then they dated. Why hadn't it worked out? I hated that I'd never asked him about his past. I'd always been too fearful of the questions that would bring up about me, so I'd avoided it. I couldn't do that anymore.

"So . . . Jaime."

Jack chuckled. "I knew we were going to have to go there."

"We don't have to." Who was I kidding? If I didn't go there, the idea of him and her together would drive me crazy.

Jack's mom leaned out the back door, calling out to Jack. "You need to get back in here." She smiled at me, the ever-friendly hostess.

"Coming."

The door snapped closed, and Jack sighed. "I'm sorry. Can we talk about this later?"

I nodded. This party couldn't be over soon enough.

"Let's go dance," Jack whispered as we walked inside.

"But doesn't your mom want you to talk to people?"

"She won't care as long as I'm visible. Besides, the only person I want to talk to is you."

He took my hand and led me to the middle of the great room and pulled me in. The music had slowed. A spooky sounding orchestra, something I never thought I'd like so much, gave us a nice melancholy beat to hold each other tight.

I breathed in his spiced citrus scent and laid my head on his shoulder. My eyes fluttered closed. Only he and I were in this moment, and I reveled in it. His hands stroked my back, sending waves of warmth cascading down my body.

When the song ended, another faster one started. Jack pulled away and spun me, showing me moves I didn't know he had. I giggled as I stumbled to keep up with him. Our moves rarely fit with the music, but it didn't take away from the fun.

James, Jack's dad, stepped next to Jack and cleared his throat. "May I cut in?"

"Of course." Jack bowed to me and stepped away.

James placed his hand at my waist and took my hand, very proper. "Are you enjoying yourself tonight?"

"I am. Thank you for having me."

"No need to thank us. We were thrilled when Jack said you'd make it."

"I don't think many expected me here," I said, noticing still eyes trained on me.

"You're right about that. He doesn't bring girls home."

"Never?" I asked before I could stop myself. His dad was probably the worst person I could have asked that.

"Well, there was one."

"Jaime, right?"

"Jaime? Oh, no, no. Sheesh, I'd forgotten those two even had a thing. This was after Jaime. I think she was the one who ruined bringing home girls for him. Money-hungry little thing. I could tell from the moment I saw her. You get pretty good at that by the time you're my age." He chuckled. "It's just too bad it took him a little longer. Really tore him up."

My stomach knotted, and then almost as immediately, I felt anger. How could someone do that to him? Cozy up to him just because he had money? It all made sense—the hidden identity, not bringing anyone to meet his family, working all the time. This girl had really done a number on him, and I hated her for it.

"Don't worry. I think you are exactly what he needs. You don't have a gold-digging bone in your body."

"How are you so sure?" I asked.

He tapped his temple, with a smirk very similar to Jack's. "I just know."

I eyed Jack chatting away, and I felt lucky to be there with him.

By the end of the night, my feet were killing me, and my stomach was so full of appetizers that my dress had tightened even more. If I even tried to sit down, I was sure it might split down the seam.

Only a few people remained when Jack said he was ready to go.

"Shouldn't we stay to help clean up?" Though, as I looked around, there wasn't a single discarded dish or cup.

"My mother hires staff for that," he whispered.

"Oh."

"Let's go say goodbye."

It was another fifteen minutes before we were able to peel ourselves away from those who were talking to his mom and dad. I didn't catch their names, but the woman eyed me around her husband in a very odd way. Maybe she too was just curious about the girl who had managed to get Jack to bring her to a family event. I was too tired to even care if it was something else. It didn't help that my mind was still preoccupied. Jaime's hand on Jack's arm kept coming forward. How often had it been there? Was she always that way, or was Jack different to her? And this other mystery woman who had broken him. Did I even dare ask about her? Did I even have a right when he knew nothing of my past?

Jack placed his hand on my lower back, bringing me back to reality. "It was so good to see you again, Ann, Bryant." He nodded his head to each. "We should go, I have to get the princess home before she turns into a pumpkin!"

Everyone chuckled at his joke. I smiled and nodded to each of them, then turned to his parents. "Thank you for having me, Mrs. Bridges."

"Oh, for heaven's sake, I thought we'd been through this. Call me Ruth."

"Ruth." I smiled.

She pulled me in for a hug, and Jack's dad winked as Jack guided me to the door.

It felt like a relief to be in the comfort of his car. I'd been under a microscope all night with how many people eyed me on Jack's arm. And now that we were alone, I could hear all about Jaime and the mystery girl. Even if I didn't like what I heard, I wanted to know it all. Though, without seeming too eager, I didn't know how to bring it up.

"Did you have a good time?" he asked.

"Yeah, your mom really does go all-out. Everyone kept staring though."

"Sorry about that. I know most of them were just curious about this gorgeous girl." He tapped the back of my hand he held.

"Psh, I'm sure that's exactly what they were thinking." I rolled my eyes.

"Well, it's what *I* was thinking."

My stomach flopped, much like it often did when he complimented me.

"I really love this costume." I fanned out the fabric in my lap. "Except when I have to go to the bathroom."

He laughed. "I'm not even going to ask."

"Actually, Jaime gave me a tip that helped a lot."

"That was nice of her."

"Uh huh." I waited, hopeful he would catch where I was headed without me having to spell it out for him. But either he wasn't enthused about talking about her, or he truly didn't get it.

The silence dragged on, it seemed like eons, but it'd only been two minutes. I could finally take no more. "So, about Jaime . . ." I let her name hang there, a question in itself.

"Oh yeah, we got interrupted." He paused as he changed lanes. "Jaime's family has always been close to ours, going back to my grandparents. So, even from birth, we were playmates. We went through a phase when I was, like, sixteen or seventeen, where we dated for, like, six months. Took us that long to figure out that we didn't belong together. She's always been more like a sister to me." He shuddered. "I still don't know what we were thinking for even that long."

"So, there's no feelings?" I asked.

"Heck no." His hand found mine amongst the thick material in my lap. "The only person I have feelings for is you." He pulled my hand to his mouth, resting his lips on my skin.

"Okay." I still wasn't convinced there was none from her end, but I decided to drop it.

The car fell silent as I contemplated how to bring up the other woman I couldn't stop thinking about. I stole a glance at Jack, his broad jaw set as he focused on the road ahead.

"Your dad told me about the girl who made you question bringing anyone to meet them." I hoped my casual tone would make things lighter.

"What? Why would he bring that up?" He was immediately on edge.

I winced. "Uh, I don't know."

"He had no right to do that!" His voice was sharp in a way I'd never heard it before. He released my hand and gripped the wheel with both hands.

I tried not to let it bother me, but it did. "I'm sorry." My voice barely above a whisper.

I could see his head turn in my direction, then he pulled the car over to the side of the road. Not a single streetlight could be seen, but I could just make out his face in the glow from the gauges on the dashboard. His anger was there in his clenched jaw, but with it, a softness was spreading across his features.

He reached back across the space between us and took my hand. "Annabelle was almost my fiancée." He closed his eyes, as if just the thought of the memory caused him pain. "Thankfully, I found out the truth about her before I proposed, or I may have never known her true intentions. You see, she let it slip to her best friend that she couldn't wait to do all these things on my dime and even had the nerve to call me what's-his-face to her. What she didn't realize was that best friend was Jaime's cousin."

I nodded. "I'm sorry."

He shook his head. "She means nothing now, just a distant memory of a bad mistake. My dad tried to warn me about her . . . wait, is that why he brought this up? Did he say something to you about your intentions?" His face changed so quickly, to concern and worry.

"No, actually the opposite. He said I didn't have a gold-digging bone in my body. He thinks I'm just what you need."

Jack sat back in his seat and stared blankly at me. "He said that?"

"Yeah."

He offered a smile, then pulled the car back onto the road, my hand clutched tighter than before.

# Chapter TEN

**LATE ONE NOVEMBER** night, when Jack and I came out of the movies, there was a missed call from Grace. Though, when I called her back from the car, she didn't answer.

Jack walked me to the door, and we were greeted by a suitcase sitting on my doorstep.

"What in the world?"

"There's a note." Jack pointed.

*Since someone ignored my call and they weren't here for my surprise, I went to the club to wait.*

*Don't wait up!*

*Grace*

"She really is full of surprises," Jack said, laughing.

"That's Grace. I'm so excited to see her." I bounced on my toes. "Will you help me bring all this in?"

"Sure. *Oof*, this weighs a ton!"

I shoved the door open and held it for him to come in.

He dropped the bag just inside the door and kicked it shut. "Does this mean I get to hang out until she comes back?"

He grinned at me eagerly, urging me to say yes. Like it really took convincing.

"Oh, you think you get to stay, huh?"

He nodded.

"And what do you suggest we do while we wait?"

He grabbed me by the waist and pulled me in. His lips found mine like a magnet drawn to the fridge. I held my breath, letting the warmth of his touch spread through my body.

My hands found their way around his back and slid upwards, drawing him in closer. His straining muscles of his back lured me to feel them better. I pushed my hands under his shirt and relished his warm, bare skin on my arms.

Behind Jack, the door sprang open, knocking against the wall, jarring me back to reality.

"It's about time . . . oh . . . uh, I'll just wait out here. Take your time." The naughty grin lit up Grace's face, and she slowly started to shut the door.

I laughed against Jack's lips. "Stop!"

Jack spun away from me, and I could see all of Grace when realization struck. I staggered.

"Grace! You're standing!"

"I know." Her voice paled in comparison to her normal loud tone. She was proud, and emotional.

I threw myself at her, careful not to knock her over. "How long have you been walking?"

"A little while now, but completely without the wheelchair for a few days."

"That's seriously the best news I've heard in a long time. I'm so excited for you."

"Me too. What's up, Jack?"

Jack nodded in her direction. "Two legs looks good on you."

"They do, don't they?"

"I will say, I think I'll miss seeing those wheelchair dance moves though," I said.

"They were pretty good, weren't they?" She giggled. "Wow, you've really come a long way since the last time I was here. A whole living room now!"

"Yep, finally got all that a few weeks ago. Jack wouldn't stop teasing me about my floor pillow furniture."

"That's because floor pillows are not furniture."

"Exactly!" Jack chimed in.

I stuck my tongue out at the two of them.

"So, where am I sleeping?" Grace asked as she dropped onto the couch.

"Right there?" I said. "Unless you want me to pull out the air mattress you slept on before?"

"Nope this is good." She settled herself down further into the cushions. "This is a really comfortable couch. Did you know that?"

"Ah, yep." I laughed.

"That's because I helped pick it out." Jack puffed out his chest.

I shoved his shoulder. "Oh hush, nobody asked you."

"Mmm, I'm so tired. I'm just going to fall asleep now, okay? Night-night."

"Okay." I giggled, flipping off the light.

The next morning, I woke to Grace in my bed, staring at me.

"Whoa," I groaned. "Why are you already awake?"

"Early bird, remember? Already done with all my exercises, and you're still asleep."

"Yes, because it's the weekend, and on weekends, normal people sleep in."

Air whooshed from her mouth. "Listen to that snark! You sound like me."

"I'd think you'd be proud."

"I kind of am." She leaned back against my wall, dazing for a minute.

But it gave me the chance to wake myself up more. I rubbed my eyes.

"Come on." She slapped the bed. "Let's go!"

Not long enough.

"Where are we going?" I knew better than to try to plan anything when Grace came to town. She always had ideas that kept things interesting.

"Shopping! I haven't been this excited to try on new clothes in forever."

"Okay, but I need coffee first."

"Duh. That's the first stop." She jumped up and smacked my butt through the covers on her way out of the bed. "Hurry, I'm ready and waiting!"

I threw back the covers and pried myself out of bed.

We hit the coffeehouse on the way to the closest mall. I got to the counter, and Jack stood up from behind it, yelling something about being out to someone in back.

"What can I get you guys?" he said, turning. And then his face lit up. "Hey."

"Hey, you. I didn't know you were going to be here this morning."

He leaned over the counter to give me a quick peck.

"Aww," Grace purred. "You didn't tell me he worked at the coffeehouse too."

Jack shook his head, trying to hold back a smile. "Hadn't planned on it, but they were having some issues with some things, so I figured it would be easier just to come in. Where are you guys off to?"

"Shopping," Grace said.

He raised his eyebrows. "Fun."

"Anything with me is fun." Grace grinned. "But first, I need caffeine. Large mocha, please."

He turned back to me. "White mocha?"

I nodded.

He called our drink orders over to the barista working at the bar, then came around the counter and put his arm around me and hung with us until our paper cups were slid onto the hand-off counter.

"If you want to cancel for tonight, don't worry about it," Jack whispered in my ear.

"No, no, but do you mind if she joins us?"

"Of course not."

"I think she'll really like that place."

"Mmm. This is exactly what I needed." Grace closed her eyes, savoring her coffee.

I kissed Jack and turned to leave. Grace followed, making kissing noises in Jack's direction.

"Bye, honey bunny," she called.

I turned in time to see him shaking his head. Not many could resist her humor.

By the third store, it became apparent Grace wanted to try almost everything on. Well, maybe I was being dramatic, but she seemed to take twice as long as me in there, which had me wondering if she was sitting for a lot of the time, resting. I wouldn't blame her if she needed to, but I doubted she'd ever admit it. She was too proud.

"Hey, should we take a break and get something to eat?" I suggested.

"Oh, yeah. I'm starved."

"So, what made you decide to come out so suddenly?"

She opened the door and looked at me with an arm full. "What? You aren't happy I came?"

"Of course I am. I'd never turn away a visit from you, but I was just wondering if there was more to it."

She groaned. "You know I don't like talking about depressing crap."

"Yes, I do, which is why I asked."

She was quiet the entire time we ordered our food until we sat and started eating. I gave her the time she needed, knowing her quiet meant she was thinking.

"My parents threatened to kick me out when I told them I wanted to come visit now that I can walk."

"Why would they care? It's just a few days."

She didn't lift her eyes from her plate, but I could see her bite her lip. "I'm technically not supposed to be without the wheelchair yet."

"*Grace!*"

"I'm fine! They're just being overprotective."

"They love you."

"I know they do, but nobody knows what it's like to have something like your leg function taken away. Now that it's back, I never want to go back to that chair."

"I don't blame you, but if the doctor's . . ."

She glared at me.

"Look, you aren't going to like what I'm going to say," I started.

"Then don't say it."

"*But* I had to do a lot too when I was recovering. I can understand wanting to just be yourself all over again. If anyone can understand that, it's me. I may not be limited physically anymore, but you know how much this memory thing has held me back."

She crossed her arms, but she didn't argue.

"Everyone just wants you to have everything back, but why risk it if you aren't supposed to be up all the time? Is the freedom really that hard to wait for that you're willing to risk losing it all?"

She didn't answer.

"Grace."

"I get it, okay? I just wanted one weekend. I couldn't even last two days."

"What do you mean?"

"Do you really think it takes me that long to change?" She cocked her head to the side.

"You need to call your parents."

She stuck her tongue out at me. "I will. Tonight, when my plane lands."

"You fly out tonight? Already?"

She nodded. "I told you I only wanted a weekend. It was short, so I figured it would be fine."

"Are they going to let you come home?"

She shrugged. "I doubt they'll actually kick me out."

"Good. Let me know either way."

"Fine. Can we be done with this . . . yuck, please?"

"Yes. When does your plane leave?"

She looked at her phone. "Three hours."

"Grace! You hardly gave us any time to get there!"

"What? I didn't really want to go back."

I shook my head.

We rounded the airport an hour later, with all her bags in tow.

"Good luck."

"Thanks."

"I'm really glad you came."

"Me too. And for what it's worth, you're so much happier with Jack. I never saw you smile as big as you did when he was with you."

"Thanks."

She gave me a quick squeeze and let go.

"Blech." She shook like a shiver had run through her whole body. "I hate that mushy stuff."

"Don't forget to call me when you talk to your parents. I mean it."

She gave me a thumbs up and shut the door.

She never called, but I did get a thumbs-up text from her later that night while I was cozied up on my couch with Jack. Her way of avoiding talking about hard things, but at least I knew she was back home where she belonged.

I snuggled deeper into him, focusing all my attention on the movie in front of us.

The next thing I knew, someone was rubbing my back, coaxing me awake. His soothing voice tickled my ear. "Wake up."

"Jack?" I mumbled.

He kissed my forehead. "It's time to get up, beautiful."

"What time is it?" I searched the darkness for a clock, coming up empty. "The sun isn't up."

"Almost. You've got to get up." He waved a steaming paper cup in front of me. The smell of coffee hit me, tricking my brain into waking up more for the warm reward.

My mind couldn't comprehend why he would be here, let alone waking me up before the sun, but I pulled myself up and reached for the coffee.

"What are we doing?"

"Just get dressed. Dress warm, it's chilly." He lifted me from the couch and guided me towards the stairs.

I dressed, moving only as fast as my sleepy body would allow, my curiosity growing the more I awoke.

Jack was waiting at the front door when I emerged from my room. "Ready?"

"I don't know. What do I need to be ready for?"

A grin lit up his face. He relished keeping this unexpected surprise from me.

He opened the door and gestured for me to go ahead of him.

"You aren't going to tell me, are you?"

He leaned forward and kissed my cheek. "Nope."

The street was silent, all businesses closed and dark. There wasn't a single car in sight.

I shivered against the cold leather seat in Jack's car. As if anticipating my cold, he reached forward and switched on the heated seat. Before long, the crisp cold was just a memory.

The car swung away from my street, then away from the city, leaving the lights hidden behind the tall tree branches of the forest. Not a single light shone in our rearview.

Jack turned the car off the highway onto a dirt road. It ended shortly in an empty parking lot. He stopped the car in the closest place next to the trailhead.

"We're going hiking?"

"Sort of."

"Sort of." I eyed him.

He made to zip his lips and got out. He'd pulled a basket out of his trunk before I'd even exited. I followed him to the opening between two huge boulders and glanced down at my shoes.

"You didn't tell me to wear hiking shoes."

"Those will be fine." He grabbed my hand and pulled me along.

The trail itself wasn't much different than walking on a sidewalk—it was firmly packed, with not many rocks or debris. The darkness that surrounded us was a little creepy at times. It felt like there were eyes on us, though we couldn't see them.

When the sky began to lighten, the trail gave way to a flattened mountaintop. It was still too dark to see anything below, but I couldn't wait to see the view when the sun rose. And then it hit me as I watched Jack spread a blanket on the ground.

A smile crept up on my face, and I crossed my arms. "Mister Bridges, did you wake me up at a god-awful hour to go on a hike so we could watch the sunrise?"

"Maybe." He patted the blanket next to him and pulled out a thermos. "I may have also brought your favorite coffee."

"You're the best."

He handed me the lid of the thermos, filled with creamy white chocolatey warmth. It couldn't get much better. And then he proved me wrong when he placed a blueberry scone in my hand.

"Mmm, breakfast too. What did I do to deserve this?"

He leaned over and put his arm around me. "You don't have to do anything. You deserve the world."

The sun brightened the horizon. Slowly it rose from just peeking out, to fully exposed, casting light out onto everything below. The view below was breathtaking, more than I could have imagined.

"How did you find this place?" I asked.

"I think I've hiked every trail within a thirty-mile radius."

"Really?"

He nodded. "Before I met you, work was the only thing that occupied my time. I needed something to blow off steam."

"You'll have to show me some."

"This one . . ." He paused. "This is where I come to think."

"It's amazing. I usually just go into the woods behind my house."

"Anything good back there?" He leaned back on his hands, watching me rather than the sunrise.

"There's a stream. I like to sit on this rock and watch it. I haven't gone much further than that though."

"With all the time I've spent at the coffeehouse, I don't know why I never thought to go back there."

"Probably because when you went hiking, it was to think, to get away from all influences, but back there. . ." I shook my head. "It's too close."

I looked at him, wondering if I was getting my point across. He just nodded. "You're right."

I laid my head on his shoulder as the sky turned golden. Birds around us seemed to come to life the second the light touched their tree, their sweet song surrounding us.

Then voices carried up to us. Others wanting to take in the sights early in the morning.

I sat up quickly. "Should we go?"

"Nah, they can move around us."

I moved so I could put my back against his chest and leaned back, relaxing into him, stealing all the warmth I could from him.

"Are you cold?"

I nodded. "Once the coffee was gone, the cold started coming on."

He reached for the basket and pulled out a blanket, wrapping it around me. His hands rubbed my arms until the blanket warmed.

"Thanks for bringing me here. I love watching the sunrise."

My experience watching the sunrise was a mystery to me, but I was sure, no matter the previous encounters, nothing could ever compete with this. Watching the sun fill in the darkness between the trees and valleys, with Jack by my side, couldn't be rivaled. Nothing could make this moment better. I sighed.

He mimicked my sigh with a dramatic display, falling over and taking me with him. I couldn't contain my laughter as I fell backwards. My head fell back to look at him, and I caught sight of three people just coming up over the ridge, staring at us like we'd just sprouted a new body part right in front of them.

My mouth clamped shut, and I pulled myself upright, turning back to look at them right side up. "Hi."

They smiled, nodding, but continued over to the edge to look out at the view. Jack righted himself and picked up things around the blanket, stuffing them back into the basket before settling again. He gently pulled me back against him, still chucking, and kissed the top of my head.

"Have I told you lately how glad I am you decided to give this a go?"

"Nope, you haven't." I grinned, knowing he couldn't see it anyway.

"No? Well then, you should know I haven't had this much fun in my life for so long. I needed you more than you'll probably ever know."

My heart melted at his words. Not only had he gone through the trouble of pulling together this incredibly romantic sunrise together, but his words hit me right in the heart.

"I love you," he whispered against the back of my head. His words sent a shiver down my back, and a warmth spread through me.

I turned to look at him, surprised at his words, but knowing I felt the same. I knew it more than I knew anything else.

"I love you too."

His lips were on mine, and my breath hitched. He loved *me*. This man who pursued me in the beginning before even knowing me. Who was successful beyond his years, yet still brought me coffee every morning, just because. How did I get so lucky?

His hand pressed into my back, pulling me closer. He pulled back slowly, pressing his forehead to mine. "You've made my day, do you know that, Melanie?"

"No, but you've certainly made mine."

# Chapter ELEVEN

**THANKSGIVING APPROACHED FASTER** than I ever could have imagined. It was something I'd been dreading. My mom and dad had both texted and called to check in, to see if I would be coming, both making it obvious they wanted me there. Now it was staring me in the face, and I still hadn't decided if I wanted to go.

My stress level about the decision was higher than I'd like while I sorted the files in front of me. I sighed as I placed the stack back in the file cabinet.

"What's up?" Cindy came up behind me.

"Huh?"

"You sighed. What's wrong?"

"Oh. I've just been thinking about Thanksgiving."

"I take it you aren't excited."

"Not really. I've been trying to decide if I should go home for Thanksgiving or not."

"Go," Jack said as he came out of his office. "I've been telling her. She's thinking too much."

I stuck my tongue out at Jack before turning back to Cindy. "My parents are a little much sometimes."

"Aren't they all?"

"I guess so." She wasn't wrong, but she had no idea. Nobody did, though it wasn't their fault I'd never told them about my accident. "I think I'd rather just stay home. The thought of fighting the crowds at the airport . . ." I shuddered.

"I don't blame you there." Cindy nodded. "I refuse to travel by plane during big holidays."

"See?" I pointed to Cindy but made big eyes at Jack.

"You're giving her ammunition."

Cindy shrugged. "Sorry."

Jack went back to his office with a new stack of work, and Cindy turned back to me. "If you decide to stay, you can come to my house if you want. We always have tons of people and way more food than we can eat."

"Thanks."

In the end, I decided to stay home. I know my parents were disappointed, but the truth was, I felt more at home here. I didn't really know them well enough to miss them. Jack had multiple Thanksgiving dinners to go to, but I declined when he'd invited me along. I was actually looking forward to being alone.

"Are you sure?" he asked at breakfast, Thanksgiving morning.

"Yes."

"But you'll be all alone," Jack argued.

"And I'll be just fine. I'll probably binge-watch chick flicks and eat junk food. Honestly, it sounds really relaxing."

"I guess so."

The look on his face told me he wasn't sold on the idea, but he'd accepted it. He brought me back to my place and started to get out.

"No, you don't have to walk me in. You've got a lunch to get to, I'll be fine."

"What kind of boyfriend would I be if I didn't walk you in?"

"You just want a goodbye kiss," I teased.

"Well, being a gentleman does have its perks."

"A gentleman, huh? And still expecting a kiss." I rubbed my chin and narrowed my eyes.

*** 

Thanksgiving came and went in a flourish of calories, not by any means from traditional fare either. December set in, and Christmas was rapidly approaching. Grace was calling more frequently than usual, and when she did, like now, she talked endlessly about moving near me early into the new year, after Christmas and once her family got more comfortable with the idea of her walking. And I knew she wouldn't admit it, but the real factor was her getting stronger and able to handle walking, unassisted, for longer periods of time. Regardless, the very idea of it had me excited.

"I've been looking into the community college that's only ten minutes from where you live, and it has the vet program I want to do," she said.

"You've decided, then? To go to vet school, I mean?" I asked.

"Yeah, I may be walking again, but I'm certainly never going to be able to ride again."

"Next best thing."

"Exactly. I'm starting to get excited about it. I never thought I would, but I am."

"That's really great, Grace."

"I know."

"Have you looked at any more apartments?"

"Not much. But you know, there's a lot of good real estate, much better than what you were looking at when you moved."

"Hey! I love my house."

"Oh, it's cute and all, but I'm so not willing to do all the work you did."

"It wasn't that bad." Though, thinking about her trying to do the work herself made me glad she was finding other options. Physically, I doubted she was up for it just yet.

"Keep telling yourself that."

"How are the parents handling your decision to move?"

"They're finally on board. And willing to pay for my rent while I'm in school."

"Wow, that's a big turnaround!"

"Told ya they would. It just takes them time." There was some noise in the background. "Hey, I got to go."

"Everything okay?"

"Oh, yeah. Talk soon." And she was gone.

Was that a man's voice in the background? I shook my head. *Probably her dad.*

I settled back into the couch and un-paused the movie I'd been watching when she called. Thoughts of her moving captivated my mind more. Then I remembered; I still had boxes from moving in my garage. Maybe that's what I should be doing instead of watching a movie, when I couldn't focus on it anyway. I flipped it off and headed to the garage.

Winter air seeped its way into my insulated garage, and I shivered against the cold. I spotted the boxes, realizing they were the only things keeping me from parking in the garage, and cursed myself for not getting to them sooner. After lugging them inside, I made myself a steaming mug of hot chocolate to warm my hands before I dug in.

I settled the boxes in front of me on the couch, starting with the lighter of them. I pulled out my puffy winter jacket and tossed it and the rest of the clothes I'd forgotten about in the wash, thankful for a few warmer things to add to my wardrobe.

When I moved on, I remembered the photo albums I'd thrown in. For a while, I lost myself in the pictures. Though, still nothing stood out to me.

As I grabbed the last one, I realized it wasn't a photo album at all; it was a sketchbook. Drawings of dresses, and what looked like dance costumes, filled the pages. They were really pretty. I couldn't imagine having drawn them, yet my initials were signed at the bottom of every single one.

How did I not know about this?

Neither Jeremy nor my parents had ever mentioned it. Did they even know?

I texted Jeremy. *I can draw? Why didn't you tell me?*

Thumbing through them all again, I took my time, envying each and every intricate detail that must have taken me ages to perfect.

I jumped when my phone vibrated in my lap. *I don't know. I thought you knew.*

I shook my head. *I don't remember anything.*

His response came fast now, the little dots showing me right away he was typing. *I'm sorry. I should have told you.*

I shook my head. *Not your job. Why was I drawing dance clothes? Do I dance too?*

I tried to imagine wearing one of them, but I didn't have a graceful bone in my body. Did they even let you be a dancer if you tripped on air often?

*For Emily.* His words caught me by surprise.

I'd designed costumes for Emily? It didn't feel real, yet the proof was right there in front of me. Though now, looking over it all, I had the overwhelming desire to put the pencil to paper again, just to see if I still could.

It was midnight before I looked up from the page, the box of things to my left forgotten. I stared down at the little blue dress I'd drawn. I imagined it would fall to just above the knee, flowy at the bottom, yet cinched at the waist. The rounded neckline gave way to sleeves that hugged the arms down to just above the elbow. The last touch, my favorite, was a simple white sash, tied at the waist, with a rhinestone broach at the hip. It wasn't as elegant as the ones before; however, it was perfect for what I'd wear now on a date with Jack.

I smiled to myself and grabbed my keys. Thank goodness for twenty-four hour superstores.

I loaded my cart with fabric and thread and headed to the sewing machines, determined to make this happen, even if I had no idea what I was doing.

Back at home, I pulled my new machine out of the box and set it on the new card table I bought just for this. There were so many knobs and things, I didn't even know where to start. I sat there for a while, the instruction book in my hand, looking back and forth between the two, when a thought struck me.

The book.

I raced upstairs and grabbed the single book left discarded in my bookshelf. *A Guide to Sewing.* The first time I saw it, I thought it was kind of funny it was the only thing left in a house that was in such disarray. Now I wondered if this book had been meant for me all along, like it was waiting for me, trying to tell me something. Something nothing else could, waiting for just the right moment. Now.

Using a combination of the book and machine's instructions, I cut and pinned, until I thought it was exactly the dress I'd drawn, and hopefully the right size—I'd used my own clothes as a guide.

Sewing was a lot easier than the rest. It was like my hands knew what to do before even I did. My eyes began to droop in the last few sections, and I was sure a few of the stitches showed that in their crooked way.

I held the finished product up to my body, in front of the full-length mirror in my bedroom as the sun rose, pouring sunlight into the room. Nothing gave me such satisfaction than this feeling right now, that I completed something just for me, by myself, and it was a success.

I laid it out gently on my dresser, sprawled out on my bed, and was asleep before I could even cover up.

For hours, I dreamt of lace and pins, waking with the same excitement I'd fallen asleep with, except now it had started to take shape. I wanted to design clothes. Different ideas popped into my head, and I couldn't wait to draw them out on paper.

This was my calling. I didn't need my memory to know that, and suddenly the business degree made sense. I had the design capability school couldn't give me, but the know-how to run a business—that was the tricky part. Why I'd never decided to ask my parents or Jeremy why I wanted to go to business school eluded me, but in a sense, I was glad I hadn't. This would never have been such a success to me if I knew someone else had opinions about it. Not when I was so unsure of anything before the accident.

I couldn't wait to tell Jack.

As if he knew I was thinking of him, my phone rang.

"Hello?"

"Hey babe, what are you doing?"

"Uh, I just woke up."

"What? It's one o'clock."

"Yeah, I was kind of up all night."

"Why?"

"It's a surprise." I grinned to myself.

"Okay . . ."

"What are you doing?"

"I'm headed home from the office."

"I thought you were working late?"

"I changed my mind. All the numbers are blurring together, too many late nights this week." He sighed. "Anyway, I was wondering if you want to come over for dinner?"

"Oooh, I get you and dinner cooked for me?"

His breathy chuckle echoed in the phone. "I guess so."

"What time?"

"Five?"

"See you then."

Dropping my phone to the bed, I sat there for a moment, smiling to myself like an idiot. No matter how many times we were together, or how often, I still got jitters in my stomach at the thought of seeing him. And it didn't hurt that I had such exciting news to share with him.

A few hours later, I pulled up in front of his house, dressed in the flowy blue dress, my blonde hair curled into waves.

"Jack," I called into his house. "I'm here."

I slipped out of my jacket in the doorway and hung it on the hook. The warmth of his house settled into my bones, and I shivered. A dress in this cold may not have been the best idea.

Music drifted to me, and I smiled at the romantic melody. Making my way to the kitchen, where I heard movement, I sniffed the air. *Mmm.* It smelled so good.

I stopped before I fully came into the kitchen and peeked around the corner. Jack was bent over the stove, tasting the pasta sauce. He added a little more of some seasoning I couldn't see before he nodded to himself.

I giggled, and he whipped around.

"Hey! When did you get here?"

"Just now."

"Come here." He hooked his finger in my direction and puckered his lips. He looked like a duck.

"No." I smirked.

"No?"

I shook my head, snickering. Dropping my purse where I stood and kicking off my heels, I took off running through the house. I don't know what came over me, but I wanted to have some fun teasing him. Maybe it was the cozy atmosphere or excitement of my news, but I was in a playful mood.

His loud footsteps echoed off the walls as he chased after me. I'd almost made a full circle around the main parts of the house when I came to the living room. I threw myself on the couch and hid. Not well enough, because as soon as he came bursting into the room, he stopped and listened. All was silent aside from my heavy breathing I muffled into the couch. All at once, he launched himself on top of me and attacked me with tickles.

"Eeee!" I squealed and flipped over beneath him. "I give! I give!" I puckered up just as he had before, certain I looked the same, like a duck.

A victorious smirk spread across his face as he bent and kissed me. Then he swatted the side of my butt that hung off the couch and headed to the kitchen.

"Hopefully, you didn't make me burn dinner," he teased.

I followed him and found the dining room table set for two with candles in the center. I sat down and watched him finish up.

"What's the special occasion?" I asked.

"It's been three months since you said you'd give this a chance. It's been the best three months of my life. *That* is worth celebrating."

Guilt hit me with a force that could have knocked me over. I didn't know that. How had I not realized? I couldn't even recall what day that had been on. That was the type of thing girls remembered and celebrated more often than guys. What a terrible girlfriend I was. Had I always been so callous?

My news suddenly didn't seem so important.

He came over with steaming plates of pasta and dimmed the light.

"This is so sweet." I took a bite. "And oh my God, so good."

He chuckled. "I'm glad you like it. That dress is stunning, by the way; it really brings out your blue eyes."

I glanced down at the dress and blushed. "Thanks, I'm glad you like it. In fact, that's my surprise."

"Your dress?" His brows knit together.

"I made it."

"What? Stand up." The humor and disbelief in his voice made me giddy.

I stood, and he took my hand, spinning me around in front of him, taking in every angle of it. The love in his eyes was clear.

"It's amazing. I never would have guessed it wasn't name brand."

"Thanks." I sat back down.

"What in the world made you decide to make a dress?"

I thought of the sketchbook and how I didn't remember it and the fact that he didn't know anything about my memory, and my story suddenly got very difficult.

"Uh, well, I used to draw all the time, and I found one of my sketchbooks last night. So, I thought I'd see if I still had it. I couldn't wait to try to sew it once I saw what I'd created, and here it is."

"I didn't even know you knew how to sew."

"Me either. It's sort of crazy, but when I moved into my house, there was one book left by the previous owner on the bookshelf—*A Guide to Sewing*. I don't know, maybe it was a sign that I should be doing this."

"Doing what?"

"Designing clothes. Nothing ever has made me feel as accomplished as I did when I finished this." I looked down at the fabric. "And I did it all by myself."

"Of course you did. I think you'd be great at designing clothes."

"Really? It's not silly?"

"Of course not."

"Good, I'm really excited about it. It's been a while since I've been this hopeful for something, ya know?"

"Then I guess this will have to double as a celebration for your new adventure!" He stood up and leaned over inside a cabinet, pulling out a small present wrapped in all-black wrapping with a red bow.

"*What* is that?" I asked.

"Open it." He set it on the table in front of me.

I looked from the gift to Jack and back, worry creeping into my thoughts. "I didn't get you anything."

He put up his hand, stopping me. "Just open it."

I peeled off the paper and peeked inside the box. Inside lay a single picture of a beautiful cabin on the lake. The faintest touch of winter hung on the empty branches.

I picked it up and looked more closely. My eyes lifted to Jack, questioning.

Only excitement showed on his face as he watched me. "Flip it over."

On the back, scrawled in his handwriting, it read:

*Come away with me. In two weeks. Just you and me. What do you say?*

"Here?" I asked, pointing at the cabin in the picture.

He nodded.

"It's beautiful."

"Is that a yes?"

"That's a yes. I'd love to."

A wide smile spread across his face. "Good."

"Where is this?"

"The woods, about an hour from here. It's my family's cabin. It'll just be me and you, and well, the caretaker too, but she'll stay out of the way."

"The caretaker?"

"She looks after the place when we're not there. You're going to love it. It's gorgeous."

This lavish lifestyle where you had people to take care of your houses shouldn't seem so out of this world to me. It seemed to be the same way in which I grew up. Though, it got me wondering if my parents owned any other houses. Truth be told, I was sure they did. Only, I still couldn't remember any of that.

Somehow my mind fixated on my memory, or rather lack thereof, the rest of the night, forgetting all about my exciting new adventure. Maybe it was the guilt of not having told Jack yet. There had only been a few times where the lack of a story had really been a problem, all of which I'd been quick to change the subject. I knew I had to tell him, but the longer I waited, the harder it became.

Later that night, the moment I walked through my front door, I called Grace, excited to share the news of our upcoming trip and my dress-making success with her.

"What's up?" Grace answered.

"I have news!" I squealed.

"Ooh, what?"

"Do you want the Jack news or work news first?"

"Work news, huh? Let me hear that."

"So, I was going through a box in my garage, and I found a sketchbook. Apparently, I can draw, like, really well. I used to design clothes, Grace."

"Wow, that's pretty cool. Hopefully, they're better than the prim and proper stuff you always wear."

I shook my head but ignored her comment. "I had to see if I could still do it, and I did. I drew a dress and sewed it last night."

"Wow, all in one night?"

"Yeah, we won't even discuss how tired I am, but I wore it to dinner with Jack tonight, and he loved it. This is what I want to do. I'm going to make clothes."

"What kind of clothes? Like, just dresses, or other things too?"

"I don't know. I mean, it looks like I've mostly done dresses and dance costumes in the past, but really, there's no limit."

"Dance costumes?" I could hear the reluctance in her voice.

"Yeah, I guess my best friend was a dancer."

"Well, I'm here to be a model if you need me, unless it's a frilly dance costume. You'll have to find someone else for *that*."

"Noted." I giggled.

"You better send me a picture of this dress you made."

"I will."

"Now, what's the Jack news?"

"He asked me to go away with him."

"Ooooh," she cooed. "Man, my best friend's really on a roll."

"I know. I'm really excited about it."

"Ah, you should be! I'm jealous. When do you go?"

"Two weeks."

"Oh man, that's so long to wait!"

"Eh, it's not that long. I'm kind of nervous though."

"Well, you wouldn't be you if you weren't." I could just see her eyes roll in my head.

"Yeah, yeah. But seriously, I think I'm going to tell him about the accident."

"I still can't believe you haven't yet."

"I know. I just didn't want to make him treat me different. And then it got harder and harder to tell him."

"As with any lie," she said pointedly.

"You aren't helping."

"Yeah, well, that's why I have my honesty policy. I'm honest about everything."

And she was. Sometimes brutally.

"I know you are."

"For what it's worth though, you should tell him. Anyway, I really should be going. I've got to go get ready for my date with my boyfriend."

"Yeah . . . wait, what? Boyfriend?? Since when?"

"Oh, just a couple of weeks."

"And you've kept that from me?? Miss 'Honesty is best'?!"

"Well, I didn't want you to think I was turning into you, you know, if he wasn't going to stick around."

"And he is?"

"It's looking that way."

A grin formed on my lips. "Wow, the Earth must have changed its axis. Grace is settling down."

"Hey, don't spread it around or anything."

"I'm happy for you."

"Me too. This whole boyfriend thing is actually pretty nice. He brings me coffee all the time. Nobody else did that."

"Pretty cool, isn't it?"

"You'd better pack something really revealing in your suitcase. Or better yet, make yourself something revealing," Grace added. "Gotta go. Don't forget, send me that picture."

"I won't."

And she hung up. She never was one to be an advocate for relationships—too much fun to settle down with just one. But there was just something different in the way she spoke that had me questioning if that had changed.

I opened my texts and sent her the picture she'd asked for, then opened my closet and started pulling out things I could bring on our weekend away, yet nothing seemed "right."

"I need to go shopping."

***

After packing and unpacking my suitcase at least twenty times, going shopping, and then deciding that what I'd picked the first, second, and even the third time wasn't good enough, I told Jack I needed to go shopping one last time. I'd even debated making some things too, but there just wasn't time to squeeze that in too. We were leaving first thing in the morning, and this was my last chance to get it right.

"Mel, you've been shopping twice already."

I meekly held up three fingers.

"Okay, you've been shopping three times in the last two weeks. How much could you possibly need? It's just the weekend."

I leaned against him in-between our cars. My hands straightened the collar on his button-up dress shirt.

"I'm just not sure if I like what I got. Last time, I promise. Besides, you still have to pack."

His hands made circles on my back as he spoke. "Five minutes, that's all it'll take. Besides, it's way more fun to be with you. Why don't you come over and help me?"

"No, I have to go shopping." I pulled away. "Besides, you'll have me to yourself all weekend."

"Can't wait." A child-like grin flitted on his face.

"Good, then move so I can go."

I gave him a quick peck on his cheek and pushed him to the side, moving him away from my car door. He held the door for me to get in, and when he shut it, I rolled the window down to say one last goodbye.

"Pushy, pushy, in such a hurry."

I stuck my tongue out.

"You aren't nervous, are you? About this weekend, I mean." His brows knit together as concern made its way to his face.

"No," I lied. Though I was pretty sure he could tell, the worry in his brow remained.

He reached in and grabbed my hand from the steering wheel. "It's going to be great, you'll see. I'll pick you up in the morning." He kissed the back of my hand and backed away.

Gripping the keys, I turned them in the ignition when a flash of something hit me.

Headlights in my face and an immediate sense of fear shook me. I froze, gasping, unsure what was flashing through my mind, as there was nothing in front of me.

The ringing in my ears was so loud, it muffled Jack's voice, and I couldn't hear a word he said.

And then, just like it began, there was nothing, and Jack's face had moved closer to mine, his hand gently stroking my cheek.

"Hey, are you okay?" Jack's soothing voice was in my ear as he leaned down into the space in the window.

"Oh, ah . . . I'm fine."

"Are you sure? Your face . . . you just looked so scared for a second there."

"Oh, yeah. Just a bit of a headache all of a sudden."

"Are you going to be all right driving? I can take you—"

"No. I'm fine. Really."

"If you're sure . . ." He trailed off.

"I'm sure." I smiled and gave him a quick peck.

He was skeptical still when he stepped away from the car; the uncertainty was etched in his creased forehead.

I smiled, backed out of the space, and drove away.

What was that? I'd never experienced anything like that since I could remember, which of course wasn't very long. Just as quick as it came to me, it was gone, and I couldn't really even picture what had me so shaken in the first place. Was there something more to it? Was it a memory trying to wiggle its way back to me? I'd read about that. Flashes of things would come and disappear, as if they'd never existed in the first place.

Whatever it was, more than likely stress, it was gone now. Not much I could do about that now. But boy, did it frustrate me.

Once I was at the store though, I realized there wasn't anything better than what I'd packed in my bags at home, or maybe I just wasn't in the mood anymore. The store didn't have that confidence I was looking for anyway. Clothes couldn't give me that, not in this situation anyway.

On my way home, I called in a Chinese food delivery. A little comfort food to calm me enough to settle in for the night.

My bags met me at the door, packed and ready to go. Between the nervous butterflies and flutters of excitement, I was feeling a little queasy. So much that I took my Chinese food up to bed and fell asleep with the half-empty boxes lying next to me.

*Pressing my face to the window, I tried to get a better look of the moon ahead. "Hurry, it's getting higher."*

*My toes tapped the floor to the beat, my angst to get there adding a bit more force with each tap.*

*"Don't worry. We'll get there, and the moon will still be there."*

*"But not as big, or bright."*

*"Look at it. It's lighting up the whole sky. It'll still be just as bright in five minutes." Jeremy flashed me his big, beautiful smile, and the whole world melted away.*

*The engine purred at a stoplight. Music blared as we danced along.*

*I bounced from side to side in my seat, watching him bang his head back and forth until the light changed to green again. We sang along at the top of our lungs until the song ended and a slow song started to play.*

*He reached over and put his hand on mine, pulling it to his lips. "I love you," he whispered against my skin. He pressed his lips to the back of my hand, sending fire through my body in the best way. I relished the way he made me feel.*

*I watched him sing along quietly to the song on the radio as he focused on the road ahead.*

143

*As we passed through the intersection, a bright light caught my attention. I turned. My breath caught in my lungs.*

*A bright light blinded me from the side, and for just a split-second, my body seized as I saw the headlights coming towards us. Fast.*

"Jeremy!"

*Time froze. Shards of glass suspended all around me as if tethered by invisible fishing line. My arms and legs lifted in defiance of gravity.*

*Then, all at once, everything caught up. My body flung back against the seat. The crunching metal and breaking glass rang out so loud, I could hear nothing else.*

*Just as quick as it began, there was nothing. Darkness.*

Covered in sweat, tears running down my face, I shot straight up.

*Jeremy.*

Everything came back to me in one blinding, emotional rush. The good, the bad, the heartbreaking. The time I ate too many marshmallows at Emily's birthday party and threw up white fluff in her back yard. I sobbed a little harder. Drawing, and even sewing. Graduating high school and walking across the stage with everyone cheering, even if not for me. And Jeremy, the sweet tender moment sharing our first "I love you," exactly as he told me it happened. It was every bit as amazing as he said, and more.

Every single memory I'd ever experienced was at my disposal in one incredible, overwhelming rush.

I tried to gulp back the knot that formed in my throat as my mom's face came into focus. Her drive to always be there for me in everything I did. She was at every single thing I asked her to be. Not hovering, not the way she had after the accident, worried I needed her there because I might forget something important, like to breathe, but there because she was one of my best supporters, right there alongside my dad.

"Oh my gosh, what have I done?" I doubled over in bed as my stomach heaved.

The last night Jeremy and I were together before the accident came to my mind, and my heart ached for him then, and for every moment we've spoken since, each like a dagger to my heart, knowing how much that must have hurt. Like being an outsider in a story he was meant to star in.

I had to go to them, all of them. I had to apologize for everything I'd done.

I thought of all the time I'd spent here, building a whole new life. I had Jack and his family, friends, a great job I loved. I had a routine. I couldn't just abandon it. But isn't that what I'd done before?

Everything was so messed up. How could I have thought moving was the way to solve all of this? All I'd done was create a bigger mess.

The stress burned at my core. I popped an antacid as if it would be more than a bandage on the real problem.

The need to get home, hug everyone, and tell them how unbelievably sorry I was kicked me into gear. I booked the next flight out from my phone.

I grabbed nothing except my purse and flew out of the driveway.

It wasn't until I was sitting still on the plane that I started to consider all the possibilities after this.

What would Jeremy say? Where would I live? Could I go back home now? Did I even *want* to?

How was Jack going to feel?

Jack.

I left home to get clarity, to find myself, hoping to get my memories back. I never dreamed that once they came back, I'd ache for home so much. For my parents. For Jeremy. And for Emily. Someone I'd completely cut off contact with, no matter how many times she called.

For months now, Grace and Jack filled those gaps, and now . . . now, I didn't know where I stood with any of them. How did everyone fit into my life now?

I was in love with Jack, yet there was a place for Jeremy there too. Like, somehow my heart grew in a matter of minutes, as I recalled everything that made me love Jeremy in the first place.

Two men. Two of the most amazing men I'd ever met.

I pushed everything aside and exited the plane.

Jeremy would be at his internship. I got a car service to bring me straight there. It was almost lunchtime when I arrived.

I jumped out and marched straight to the receptionist—the first desk on the third floor, where I knew he'd be, based on the hospital directory.

"Can I help you, Miss?" she asked in her very proper and poised voice. To me, it read snobbier than anything else. Her bun was extra tight, not a single brown hair askew. A little too much for a hospital. I mean, most of these people don't even have a back to their gowns, leaving their tail end in the breeze.

I gulped. "I'm looking for Jeremy Hawes. He's an intern?"

"Who may I tell him is here?" she asked.

"Ah . . . can you not tell him?"

Her eyebrows raised like I was some sort of threat, waiting.

"I just want to surprise him."

She hesitated, her hand hovering over the phone before she gripped it and made the call.

"Mr. Hawes?" She paused. "Someone is here to see you . . . she wouldn't say." Then she replaced it in the cradle. "He'll be right out."

I nodded and found a seat in the corner, where I could see the double doors open. I crossed and uncrossed my legs, feeling like I was sitting on pins and needles. I stood back up and paced by the window. The minutes seemed to drag on. And the watchful eye of the secretary made me more uneasy by the minute.

I jumped when I heard the double doors open. I turned, holding my breath for him to step out.

He was dressed in a white dress shirt, missing the white jacket doctors typically wore. He wasn't a doctor yet, so I knew he wouldn't get the privilege. *One day.* His tie rested against the buttons of his shirt, swaying a little as he turned towards me.

His hair was shorter now.

My stomach clenched. "Jeremy."

When his eyes fell on me, he froze as a huge smile filled his face. Then he made his way over to me in just a few huge strides.

His arms fell around me, larger and heavier than I remembered. I briefly wondered if he'd been working out.

"What are you doing here?"

I looked up into his blue eyes, tears welling up in mine.

"I remember."

"Oh my god, Melanie. Seriously?"

I nodded.

"That's huge . . . and amazing." He seemed to be lost for words. "When?"

I looked at my watch. "Four hours ago?" I raised my shoulders like I was guessing. "I jumped on a plane." I looked myself over. "I didn't even bring anything with me." I nervously giggled. "Sort of crazy, huh?"

He shook his head, eyes alight. "No. Sort of great. It's so good to see you." He turned back towards the doors and placed a finger to his lips, thinking. "Have you eaten?"

I shook my head.

He held up one finger, the same one he pressed to his lips. "Give me ten minutes." With that, he spun around and disappeared back through the doors.

I returned to the window and watched the goings-on outside. A few nurses were having a smoke break. It always puzzled me when I saw health professionals doing things they chastised patients for.

146

I turned my attention back inside the building when the sun became too bright. The receptionist must have decided I wasn't a threat and didn't look in my direction again.

The doors opened, and Jeremy jogged back over to me.

"Come on." He flashed me a guilty smile. "I took the rest of the day off."

He opened the car door for me, like he always had, then drove us to my favorite restaurant.

"You remembered." I brightened.

He squeezed my hand. "No. *You* remembered."

He let go too quickly; his fleeting touch was ingrained on my skin.

Then my thoughts drifted back to Jack and my stomach flopped, not in a good way.

"Two, please," Jeremy said to the hostess.

She seated us near a window in the crowded restaurant filled with professionals on their lunch breaks, most dressed like Jeremy. In my sweatpants and faded T-shirt, I was severely underdressed. Now I regretted not changing or, at the very least, bringing something to change into.

"How have you been? Your leg? Ribs?"

"Fine. All fine. Sometimes they hurt, but only occasionally."

"That's great." He looked at me and sighed. "I can't believe you're here."

"I know. It feels surreal." I stared at my hands on the table. "Listen, I wanted to apologize for leaving the way I did . . . I really messed things up."

"No. You did what you thought was right. Nobody can fault you for that."

"You can. I hurt you. You've always been so good to me."

He didn't make eye contact. I could tell it still stung. "I'm fine."

The waiter came over, and Jeremy ordered our lunch, just the way he always had, and he remembered all of what I liked, right down to asking for an extra side of alfredo sauce.

When the waiter left, I couldn't bring myself to look at him.

He reached across the table, taking my hand in both of his. "To be honest . . ." He wavered. "For months, all I could think of was the day your memory came back, anticipating . . . this." He squeezed my hand and scooted his chair around the table to sit right next to me. "What we had was amazing. I've missed you so much."

I turned, looking up into his blue eyes, my mouth slightly open.

He leaned down and pressed his lips to mine. I kissed him back with a tenderness I hadn't felt in months. It was familiar and comforting. My hand rested on his neck as he deepened the kiss. His tongue gently probed my lips to part. His kiss was sweet and gentle, where Jack's was eager and wistful.

*Jack!*

I pulled away, lifting my hands from his. I brought one hand to my lips. *Oh my god.*

"Is everything okay?"

I shook my head. "No. It's not." Tears filled my eyes.

"What's wrong?"

I looked up from the table, staring into his eyes. "I have a boyfriend."

"Oh." He looked away, but there was no mistaking the hurt that was there.

Since I'd been gone, Jeremy and I texted occasionally, but never had I thought it would be a good idea to tell him about Jack. We'd kept it light and only spoke about the good things, nothing too deep. Maybe that had been cowardly. And now seeing the hurt in his eyes, my heart broke a little.

"What am I supposed to do?"

"What do you mean?"

"I want to go back . . . back to before . . . to make a different choice. Stay. Maybe then, I wouldn't feel so . . . conflicted."

His face changed to concern. "Are you unhappy," he swallowed hard, "with him?"

"No." I intertwined my hands on the table. "That's the thing, I am really happy. Things . . . they're really great."

"Then it seems to me you've found your place."

"It's not that simple."

"Nothing is ever simple. Does he know you're here? With me?"

I shook my head. "I've been ignoring him since I left. To be honest, he didn't even know about the accident. Any of it."

"You didn't tell him anything?"

I shook my head.

"Why?"

"I didn't want him to look at me like my parents did. I thought it might make him treat me different."

"It might have."

"See?"

"But it would have been better than finding out like this, you disappearing."

I pulled my phone from my pocket and showed him the twenty-five missed calls.

His lips rose, and he looked down at the plate in front of him, no doubt avoiding my gaze. "You're giving this guy a heart attack."

"Maybe."

"You've got to call him back."

"I will. Later." *When I can figure out what to tell him.*

I shoved the phone back in my pocket.

We fell silent when the food came. The restaurant chatter and clinking of dishware carried on around us.

That kiss stuck with me. Confusing me.

"All right, enough. I can't take the silence. *We* don't do silence."

I looked up from my plate.

"It's not hard to see that this is difficult for you. It's not been easy for me either. Not even a little. I want you to know I'm here for you, no matter what. If you decide I'm the one for you," he grinned, "you'll make me the happiest man in the world. But if you decide that's not in the cards for us . . . well, I'll just have to accept that. Just know I expect a text at least weekly. Having you as a friend is better than not having you in my life at all."

"You're really special."

He smirked at me. "I don't know what you're talking about."

***

Jeremy stopped in front of my parents' house just as the sun started to dip lower in the sky. Looking up at the huge house, I felt small.

Only six months had passed since I lived here, yet it somehow seemed like a lifetime. I wasn't the same person who left here then, yet somehow I wasn't the same person I went to bed as last night either, leaving me once again in limbo. At least now I had knowledge and experience behind me, and it would only be until I decided where I fit best. With my family—that is, if they could forgive me for leaving? Jeremy? Or with Jack?

"Do you want me to go with you?" Jeremy asked when I didn't get out right away.

I shook my head. "I just need a minute."

How do you apologize to someone you haven't spoken to in months? Truthfully, we'd talked, once or twice, but an "I'm fine. How are you?" didn't really count. You said those things to people you passed on the street and wouldn't say you talked to them. It was the niceties most didn't even think about, yet always had an automatic response.

My mom was probably so hurt, and I couldn't blame her. No matter how close I was to my dad, she was still a huge part of my life before.

"Okay. I'm ready."

Jeremy reached for me. "Today was great catching up. I'm really glad you're back." He squeezed my hand, smiling. "Really glad. You'll call me later?"

I got out, nodding, but stopped before I shut the door. "Thanks for always being there for me."

"There's nowhere I'd rather be."

I shut the door and faced the house. Walking slowly up the walk, the sound of Jeremy pulling away from the curb made me jump.

*Stop it.*

I straightened my sweatpants and T-shirt, as if that would make me look more presentable somehow. Closing the distance in three large strides, my hair blew away from my face when I opened the door.

At first I didn't hear anyone, then a soft *clink* of glassware floated to me from the kitchen.

"Hello?" I called, making my way deeper into the house.

"Melanie?" Mom responded. Moments later, she stepped into view from the kitchen, drying her hands on an apron.

I held my arms out to my sides, then flattened them against my body. "Hi, Mom." I closed the distance, flinging myself at her. "I'm so sorry."

She gripped me. "Honey, what's wrong?"

"Nothing . . . and everything." I pulled away. "I remember everything. I've hurt everyone so much. You, Dad, Jeremy . . . I haven't even taken a single one of Emily's calls. I didn't know what to say to her, and now. . ." I sighed.

Mom reached for me, pulling me in. She said nothing, but she shook with silent sobs. My eyes burned as tears threatened. When she finally pulled away, moisture remained below her eyes, but a smile was present on her face. "My baby's back. We must call your dad. We have to celebrate."

Dad came straight home, looking like he'd just won a prize. "Where is she?"

"Right here, Dad."

He enveloped me in his arms. It was good to be here and know who I was without wondering in the back of my mind if I was being true to the person I was.

The vibration of my phone shook my purse for what seemed like the thousandth time today. I ignored it again, just like every time before.

*Not yet.*

I didn't look at the screen, which I was sure was filled with texts too, and shut it off.

Mom came into the room. Her face lit up like it always did before this whole mess began. It made me happy to see her that way. She stopped when she saw me hugging Dad and pressed her hands to her heart.

"I made reservations for dinner," she said.

"I have a better idea. Can I cook for you guys?"

I doubted my mom's jaw had ever dropped faster. Dad smiled down at me, dropping his arm to my waist.

"Make me a list. I'll go to the store," Mom said, recovering from her moment of surprise.

By eight o'clock, we sat down at the table together for the first time in months, with heaping plates of parmesan crusted chicken and asparagus risotto.

Mom looked down at the plate in front of her. I watched her take the first bite, waiting for her reaction. Her eyebrows shot up.

"Where did you learn to cook?" she asked.

I shrugged. "Cookbooks?"

"This is amazing," Dad said.

"It's Jack's fav—" I stopped myself when I realized they didn't know who Jack was.

I never told them about Jack. I don't know why. It wasn't like they would be upset, but for some reason, I felt the need to keep that part of my new life hidden. In some weird way, it seemed right. But now that I sat across the table from them, nothing but regret filled me.

"Who's Jack?" Dad sat back in his seat.

"Ah . . ." I shut one eye and scrunched my face in a grimace. "My boyfriend?"

"Oh, yeah?" Mom's eyebrows rose. "I didn't know you had a boyfriend."

"I know."

"Tell us about him."

I was relieved she wanted to know more rather than upset to have been kept in the dark.

"He owns his own business. Well, he owns multiple businesses."

Dad set his fork down and leaned back in his chair. "Really? What business?"

Touching on my dad's forte had piqued his interest.

"Uh, he's an investor. And he owns a coffeehouse."

"That's an interesting mix."

"Yeah, I guess he invested in the coffeehouse, and the owner failed miserably, so to keep it from going belly up, Jack bought him out and turned the whole place around. It's thriving now."

"That's impressive."

"Jack sounds older," Mom said. From her tone, I knew it was a question, and she didn't seem to like the thought.

"Ah, yeah, a little bit."

"What's a little bit?" Dad asked.

"Twenty-three."

Dad nodded, taking a bite. "Still fairly young for what he's accomplished, it sounds like."

I nodded.

"How did you meet?" Mom asked.

I thought back to his piercing green eyes staring at me from across the coffeehouse. The same eyes I often caught gazing at me now when I wasn't paying attention. I thought of all the time I actively avoided them, hoping to get away unseen. And of Grace, completely unaware Grace, who happened to bring him to me, wishing I'd take her bait.

"In the coffeehouse. It's on the same street as my house."

Mom smiled. "We'll have to come visit and meet him."

"Come to Colorado?" I asked.

"Of course. Unless you don't want us to?"

I thought of going back to Colorado. Going back to Jack. And it already hurt, like I was leaving behind part of myself.

And yet staying just didn't seem right, though the draw to be with the people I was most familiar with pulled at me.

I wanted both lives. I wanted both Jack and Jeremy. And as much as I loved my independence in Colorado, I also loved the warmth and comfort of being at home with my family.

Getting my memory back did nothing to change the feeling of living in two worlds. My past and my present, except now I was in love with two men, and I was drawn to both lives.

"Oh, of course. I'd love to show you my house. I've done a lot of work to it."

"Oh really, you hired a contractor?" My mom seemed surprised at this.

"Oh no, I did the work myself."

Her eyes practically bugged out of her head. "You did construction work?"

"It wasn't really construction. I refinished my staircase and painted, that kind of thing. Nothing big."

"I'm impressed," Dad said. "I have to see this handiwork. I might have to put you to work around here."

I shook my head, laughing.

"Do you have plans tomorrow?" Mom asked.

I shook my head as I shoveled another bite in my mouth.

"Would you like to go shopping? I've missed our shopping days. Maybe we can get pedicures too?"

"That sounds amazing."

"Good."

Later that night, I flipped my phone back on and read all the missed messages, mostly from Jack. He was worried sick. I couldn't say I blamed him. I'd disappeared. Ignored all his calls. And of all days, the day we were supposed to go away together.

Then one message from Jeremy caught my attention.

*I hope you aren't still ignoring your phone. It was so good to see you today. Can I see you again tomorrow? Dinner?*

I didn't even have to think for a second.

*Pick me up at 6.*

My stomach flopped with anticipation. And my phone vibrated again. Jack.

*I'm really worried, Melanie. Please call me.*

I closed my eyes and shut out the world.

# Chapter
# TWELVE

**THE NEXT MORNING,** I didn't bother to check my phone. I knew my plans for the day, and nothing would change them regardless of what was on that screen, and I was sure there was a lot.

I wasn't ready to make a choice yet. I needed time. I knew what I left behind—it was wonderful and amazing, and full of everything I wanted. The moment I spoke with Jack, I knew I wouldn't be able to think clearly. Just the sound of his voice would make me want to jump on a plane to be with him. But if memory served me right—and for once, it was—I had to figure out if that also remained here, where my parents were, where I'd grown up, where Jeremy was, that I missed so much. I owed this to myself after fleeing from everyone who mattered, and I owed it to Jeremy, but most of all, I owed it to Jack. I could never be all-in if I always wondered if there were still someone here for me.

Mom met me at the bottom of the stairs as soon as I emerged from my room, dressed. "Hungry?"

I nodded, yawning.

"Good, we'll get something to eat too."

The day slipped by so fast, I could hardly believe it when I glanced at my watch and it said 5:30 p.m. It had been so long since I'd had a good girls' day like this, and I couldn't help thinking we could do this all the time if I lived here again.

At six o'clock, Jeremy knocked at the front door. I slipped into my ballet flats and grabbed my clutch, all new from today, courtesy of my mom. When I opened the door, Jeremy's eyes slid up and down. My cheeks warmed under his scrutiny.

His eyes lit up. "You look amazing."

"Thanks. It's all new."

"I can tell. It's nothing like you used to wear."

I frowned and looked back over my outfit choice.

"In a good way," he quickly added.

He followed me to the car, rushing to get ahead of me at the last second to open the door. He held it wide, waiting for me to get settled before he shut it.

I hadn't considered what this was until that moment. Clearly, Jeremy thought it was a date.

*Is that what I wanted?*

He climbed in next to me, shaking me from my thoughts.

He drove without turning on the radio and kept his head facing forward. I hadn't noticed it yesterday when we'd spoken the entire time. I studied his tight arms. After driving a few blocks, the silence was driving me crazy.

"No music?" I asked.

He shook his head. "Haven't been able to since . . . well, you know."

"That wasn't your fault."

He didn't respond. I watched him, then reached out and flipped on the radio. Not loud, but just enough to give us something to enjoy.

He gripped the steering wheel tighter until the tops of his knuckles turned white.

I reached over, placing my hand on his arm. "Relax. It's just music."

As the minutes passed, his posture slumped more in his seat as he grew more comfortable.

"How are your parents?" I asked.

"Good. They went on a cruise a few weeks ago."

"Ooh, that sounds nice."

He nodded. "Mom's been raving about it ever since. I think she's already planning their next one."

He parked in front of an arcade that also served food and turned to me. "How's this?"

I looked up at the giant brick building. "Sounds like I'm going to get more tickets than you!"

I jumped out of the car and raced to the door, with Jeremy trailing at my heels. Once inside, we were seated at a table far from the games. The distant sound of chiming buzzers added to the loud atmosphere. We placed our drink order, and I searched the menu. I found only two things

I had to have to go with a trip to play games—nachos and a giant pretzel with cheese. I shut the menu and stared at Jeremy.

Eventually, he glanced up from the menu. A smirk formed on his lips. "What?"

"Oh, nothing. What are you going to get? *Wait!* Let me guess . . ." I put my fingers to my temples and closed my eyes. "You're going to get a bacon cheeseburger with . . . ah, onion rings!"

"You're too good."

We ordered and it seemed to take only a few minutes before the waitress returned with our food. My mouth watered.

It was heaven eating all the junk food, devouring it far faster than I thought I could.

Jeremy's eyes bugged out as I finished the last bite. "I didn't think for a second you'd finish all that."

"Me either." I dabbed my mouth with a napkin.

"Ready to play?"

A giddy buzz fueled me as I looped my arm in his and we headed into the area filled with flashing lights. A few kids ran in front of us, but mostly we were surrounded by other couples and groups of adults out for a good time, beers in hand.

Between basketball and skeeball, I seemed to hold the better skill. After three tries at each, losing each time, he suggested we move to another game, though I suspected it was because he didn't want me to beat him again. Racing, on the other hand, was exactly his game. He beat me five times in a row.

At the end of the night, our cups were overflowing with tickets. We put them in the ticket counter at the same time, and I beat him by only three tickets.

"Told ya I'd beat you," I boasted.

He rolled his eyes. "Three tickets."

"Still beat ya! What do I win?"

"Win? What? We didn't place bets."

I crossed my arms.

"Fine. How about this?" He reached out and pulled me against his body, holding me there. I was stiff at first, then I let myself relax in his arms. It felt good. Really good. He leaned back and kissed my forehead.

"That'll work," I whispered.

We stood there, locked in our embrace, until a little kid ran smack dab into us, then ran away like nothing happened. We giggled.

"We should go get our prizes."

I eyed the center display. With only a second's thought, I loaded my arms full of candy, enough to use all my tickets. Jeremy's eyes widened.

"Really?"

I cocked my head to the side. "Don't tell me the thought never crossed your mind."

He turned away with a smirk and reached for a package on the shelf.

"What's that?" I asked, leaning around him.

He held it up.

"Earbuds?"

He nodded. "Mine just broke the last time I went to the gym."

He'd been working out, as I suspected. My mind drifted to what his abs looked like now. I had to shake myself to remove the image from my mind. And what a good image it would be.

He made a lap around the prize area, with me trailing behind him. His eyes finally settled on a foam football.

He grinned and gripped it in his palm. "We should go throw this around."

I giggled at how into it he seemed. This was a side of him I loved. His playful spirit that came out at just the right times, while he remained serious and sensitive, yet happy and engaging the rest of the time.

"Sure, but only after you help me eat some of this candy."

"Deal."

After cashing in the tickets, I popped some candy in my mouth as we walked to his car.

"Should we go to the park?" he asked.

I nodded. "Definitely."

By the time we rolled into the parking lot of the park closest to my parents' house, we already had a fairly large sugar buzz going. I pulled out two of the large sugar sticks and handed one to Jeremy.

"Think we can eat it all at once?"

He eyed the tube. "I don't know."

I took the plastic between my teeth and yanked. Other than putting teeth marks in it, nothing changed. I made a face.

"Hand it over." He pulled a knife from his pocket and flipped it open, the blade glinting in the darkness. He sliced through the plastic like it was warm butter.

"Since when do you carry a pocket knife?"

"Ah . . . since the accident."

I gave him a strange look.

"My seat belt, it jammed. I couldn't get out until the firemen cut me free." He paused. "Being trapped there in my seat with you lying unconscious, without being able to do anything. . ." He shuddered. "I just don't want to ever feel like that again."

He held up the knife and cut the top off his. "Problem solved. I can free myself next time, and it's come in handy a few times already for other things." He handed me a sugar stick, smiling encouragingly.

"Hopefully, there won't be a next time."

He nodded slowly.

"Bottoms up!"

Tilting my head back, sugar filled my mouth. I watched Jeremy from the corner of my eye doing the same. He made a face at me, and I tried not to laugh but failed miserably, spewing powdery sugar all over his car in a light pink puff.

I swallowed the remnants in my mouth and turned to Jeremy, pressing my lips tight together. "Oops. . ."

He eyed the stick in my hand, the remaining sugar resting inside. Before I realized what he was thinking, he snatched it from my hand and shook the last of it over my head.

"Hey!" I yelled and jumped out.

He clutched his stomach, laughing. As I stood there, trying to glare at him, my resolve weakened and I started to crack. Before long, we were both overcome with laughter.

He used my distraction and tossed the football to me. My arms narrowly caught it in my stomach.

"Hey! I wasn't ready!"

He slid out of the car, holding out his hands once he locked the car. "Let's see what you've got."

I clutched the ball between my palms and brought back my arm. I chucked it as hard as I could. The ball tumbled end over end before it hit the ground five feet in front of him.

Dropping my face in my hands, I burst out laughing.

Jeremy chuckled like he didn't know what to say. "Ah . . . what was that?"

I threw my hands out to my sides.

He tossed it back underhand. "Try again."

I gripped the ball again, taking care to have a good hold on it, then launched it once more. This time, it arched up and flew the way it should yet still landed short.

He bent, his hands on his knees, looking at the ball on the ground.

"How did I not know this about you?" He scratched his head.

"I guess you never put a ball in my hands before." I smirked at my unintentional play at something a bit more.

Jeremy's mouth opened just a little, then he quickly shut it, nodding. "You would be correct."

We tossed the ball back and forth for a while until my arm started to ache.

I dropped down into the grass, lying on my back, staring at the stars. Jeremy lay down with me, putting his head on my stomach. It felt comfortable being this close, like an old blanket would.

"When are you going back to Colorado?"

"Mmm . . . that is the burning question, isn't it?"

Jeremy stayed quiet.

"I should . . . like, tomorrow. It's not like I called anyone . . ."

"You still haven't called . . . ah . . . what's his name?"

"Jack."

"Yeah, him."

"No."

He blew out a breath. "That's rough."

"I know, but what am I supposed to say? I got my memories back and remember my family . . . and my ex. And now I have to make sure I don't still have feelings for him?" I shook my head. "*That* would go over well."

"Is that what this is?"

My face burned. "I guess so."

He nodded. "And what have you decided?"

I looked away from his penetrating gaze as he looked up at me, expectant. "I don't know," I whispered.

"Do you feel anything for me? I just have to know before I let myself hope there's a chance." He brushed a hair away from my eye.

"I do."

He grinned, but I could tell he tried to hide it. "Okay."

He reached down and grasped my foot, his fingers rubbing in a circular motion. He worked over my whole foot, then moved to the next. I lay there, quietly enjoying his gentle touch. Then he stopped. I watched his fingers hovering less than an inch from the bottom of my foot. He wiggled them back and forth, a devilish look in his eye.

I tensed. "Don't even think about it."

"Think about what? This?" He brushed his fingertips, featherlight, across my arch.

I kicked my foot, trying to free it from his grasp, without success. He doubled his attack, with his fingers pressing harder, letting his nails slide across my skin, sending zings to all my nerves. I giggled uncontrollably. Spinning onto my knees, I crawled away, leaving him scrambling to catch up.

I stood and turned, squaring my shoulders, remembering his one weakness. The one and only place he was ticklish. Holding up my hands next to my ears, I waited. "All right. I'm ready this time!"

He stopped and smirked. "Truce!" He held up his hands.

I dropped mine back to my sides. "That's what I thought."

He threw his arm around my neck, and we walked like that back to his car.

This time, he didn't hesitate to turn the radio on low while he drove me to my parents. I smiled to myself and turned to look out the window.

Red-and-blue flashing lights met us as we pulled onto my parents' street. I blinked against the brightness and lifted my hand to block the light from burning my eyes.

My stomach plummeted the second I realized which house they were in front of.

# Chapter
# THIRTEEN

"OH MY GOD." I gasped. "What's going on?"

Jeremy pulled the car to the curb across the street, in the only place there was room. I jumped out before we even stopped moving, followed a mere seconds later by Jeremy.

The officers huddled in a small group turned, revealing the men on the other side of their group. A face I didn't expect stared back at me.

Jack.

I froze in the headlights of Jeremy's car. Jack's eyes fell on me, and his face flooded with relief, then quickly shifted to confusion when Jeremy stepped beside me. The hurt in Jack's eyes couldn't have been more obvious if he'd have yelled it out himself.

I stood there, unable to pry my eyes away, yet powerless to go to him.

For those moments, time seemed to stand still, everyone frozen around me, except Jack. His mouth moved, saying something I couldn't hear. Oh, how I wished I could. He shook hands with each of the officers. And my dad. Oh God.

His eyes left mine, flickering briefly to Jeremy before he walked away, got into a sleek sedan, and drove out of view.

Jeremy's hand on my back broke me from my trance. "You okay?"

"Huh?"

"Are you okay?"

"Ah . . . I don't know."

His brow creased.

I made my way across the street as a cold sweat broke out on my skin.

The officer's badges glistened in the light. I swallowed hard.

"What's going on?" I asked.

"Are you Melanie Avery?" One of the officers stepped forward. His stern face and hard lines raised goose bumps on my skin.

Nervously, my hands clenched together as I stepped forward next to my dad. "Yes."

"Hello, Melanie. It seems that a Mr. Jack Bridges believes you're missing."

My stomach dropped. *Missing?*

The guilt threatened to choke me. Here I was, out having a good time with Jeremy, while Jack was out searching for me. Worried about me. And then I showed up with another guy, despite ignoring his texts and calls.

Jeremy's hand still rested on my back, and it was like it was burning a hole in my skin. I shook it off. His arm brushed my side as he shoved his hand in his pocket.

"We're sorry to bother you all. Jack was adamant that something was wrong . . . ah . . ." He cleared his throat. "Since you weren't answering your phone."

I bit my lip and focused on the ground.

"It's apparent, Melanie, you're just fine."

I nodded.

The officer reached out and gripped my shoulder gently. "Give us a call if you need anything. Anything at all." He slipped his card into my hand.

"Thank you. I'm sorry you had to go through all this trouble."

"It's what we're here for, but might I suggest getting in touch with Jack."

I nodded. "I will."

The officers tipped their heads. "Goodnight, Miss. Sirs."

"Goodnight."

Wrapping my arms around myself, I stood there for a moment, watching the patrol cars' flashing lights shut off, then drive away.

Regardless of my silence, not once had it crossed my mind he would send a search party for me. Who was I to elicit so much worry?

"I'll let you two say goodbye," Dad said before turning and heading back inside.

Facing Jeremy right now was the last thing I wanted to do. My mind was a jumbled mess, and anything I said to him now might hurt him, or worse, give him more hope than I should.

"Thanks for tonight."

"Anytime," he said.

He leaned down slowly. I knew what he was doing, maybe even before he'd come any closer. At the last second, I turned my head. His lips pressed into my cheek. A very different reaction from just over twenty-four hours ago, when I'd kissed him back.

I closed my eyes, unable to face him after what I'd just done. Turning towards the house, I walked away without another look in his direction. I doubted I could have been colder, but somehow, I just didn't have anything else in me.

I tossed and turned that night, the ache in Jack's eyes haunted me in my dreams. The sting of him seeing me get out of Jeremy's car. And then of his back as he walked away from me and drove away. The way I'd frozen at the sight of him had me cringing even still.

Why did I just stand there? Why didn't I run to him? Why did I just let him go?

Jeremy's arms hadn't provided the comfort I needed. They'd only masked the pain. How could I not have seen that before? It didn't matter what we shared before, it was nothing in comparison to what I had with Jack. If it weren't for being so overwhelmed by all my memories flooding back all at once, maybe I would have seen that sooner. And none of this would have happened.

It was still dark out when I was finally able to make sense of the mess inside my head. It wasn't until then I realized where I belonged, with more clarity than I could have even hoped. I shot out of bed, snuck into my parents' room, and gently nudged my dad awake.

"Can you drive me to the airport?" I whispered.

Even half-asleep, a smile lit up his face. "I was wondering when you were going to go after him."

My mouth dropped as I stared at him.

"What? You may not have remembered me until recently, but I've never seen you as happy as when you spoke of Jack at dinner the other night. And that man loves you a great deal if he brought out that kind of response, all because you wouldn't answer your phone."

"He really does make me happy."

"Then go, *go*. Let's get you back to him so you can fix this."

As we headed out the door, the sun had begun to brighten the sky just enough to make it glow and make the stars disappear.

"I can't believe you ran home and never even called him once."

I sighed. "I know. It's even worse than that though, I really messed up."

"Worse? How could it be worse?"

"I never told him about . . . the accident or my memory."

"Oh, Melanie."

"I know. He'll probably never speak to me again, and I'll be out my job too."

"Give the guy some credit. If he makes you as happy as you say he does, then he must be a pretty good guy. Do you think he would actually fire you over this?"

"No, but I wouldn't blame him if he did."

"I would."

"*Dad.*" I rolled my eyes.

"Well, nobody can fire my little girl." He reached over and rubbed his hand on top of my arm.

Dad walked with me to the ticket counter and paid for the next flight out, even though I told him I didn't need him to.

"What kind of dad would I be?" He kissed me on the forehead as I threw myself into his arms one last time at security. "You'd better be back to visit really soon."

"Nope. I think it's your turn to come see me. . . and my house. I think you'll like it."

His face lit up. "You've got it."

"Tell Mom I love her."

"I will. Now, go on. Go get him."

I let go and walked into the security line. I turned back every so often until I couldn't see him anymore, but he stood there, watching me the whole time, unmoving.

Over and over in my head, I went through what I would say to Jack when I saw him. And though nothing seemed perfect, I doubted anything would.

All my calls went unanswered, but I knew right where he would be on a Monday morning. I drove straight to the office. His car was parked right where it always was, and I breathed in deep. "Please make him listen."

But when I opened the door and stepped inside, I was greeted by a perky blonde. I sidestepped at the blow of seeing someone else at my desk.

"Hi there, I'm Sandra. How can I help you?" She said it as if she'd always been here. At *my* desk, doing *my* job.

My heart sank. He'd already replaced me.

"Are you okay? You don't look so good." Sandra stepped closer.

"I need to speak with Ja— J.R." I said it like I'd never even been here before. Like I was asking for permission. But when her brows furrowed, I realized she had no idea who I was talking about. No surprise there.

"I know the way," I added and started walking toward his office without giving her the option of a reply. It truly wasn't up to her anyway. I'd be going back there, whether she was okay with it or not.

I threw open the door, unsure of what I'd find on the other side. Sandra was close behind me, unsure if she should object.

Cindy and Jack looked up at me, startled. Jack's face hardened when he realized it was me. It was like a knife twisted in my gut. My lip quivered.

"Miss," Sandra called from behind me.

I stepped in the office and shut the door. Outing him to his new employee wouldn't be another thing to add to the list of reasons he was mad at me.

I pressed my back to the door. "Can we talk?"

Cindy looked between us and then made her way to me. "I'm just going to go see how Sandra is doing."

I moved to the side and let her leave. My eyes never left Jack, who didn't seem to want to talk to me at all, but it meant a lot that he'd at least resisted telling Cindy to stay. I couldn't imagine trying to lay this all out in front of her too.

"I'm sorry." There was so much more I wanted to say, yet now that I stood in front of him, I froze. Nothing came.

"You're sorry? That's it? You're sorry?"

My eyes stung at the anger in his voice. "No, that's not it. But you need to know that first. Because I am *so* very sorry. Please at least listen to everything I need to say. It's a lot."

He leaned back in his seat, his hands folded over his stomach. He looked so powerful behind his huge desk. So intimidating.

I dropped into the chair across from him. "The hardest part of all of this is that I didn't confide in you before . . . the reason I moved . . . my broken leg. Six months ago, I was in a car accident. I told you that part, but I didn't tell you all of it. A car ran a red light. It T-boned us, hitting right on my door, full speed. They think the other driver fell asleep at the wheel. I guess that's not really important right now. . ." I hesitated, looking up at him.

His eyes urged me to continue.

"I didn't wake for two days. Unfortunately, when I did, I had no memory. No recollection of who I was. Everything was gone. My parents were absolute strangers."

Jack watched me, his lips tightening.

"They let me leave the hospital a few days later, but getting around with a broken leg and multiple broken ribs wasn't easy. My mom hovered a lot. *A lot.* I hated it. She kept looking at me like I might sprout another head if she looked away, and there were a few times I thought I had because I'd done something 'Melanie never would have.'"

I could see he was getting antsy, though at the same time, I could tell I'd piqued his interest because his eyes were focused.

"I was afraid to do anything. I had no freedom, except with Grace. I met her in the hospital. She felt like the only person I had. The only one I remembered from the beginning. Everyone else had all these memories of me. How could I live like that?"

"Well, it's clear I really didn't know you at all."

"That's not true. I told you from the start I couldn't get involved with anyone, and that was because I had no idea when my memories would come back, if they ever would. Let alone *how* I would feel if they did."

"So why not tell me all of this, then? Why keep it from me all this time?" He shook his head. "I feel like an idiot."

"Because I didn't want you to look at me like I was broken. You didn't know that side of me."

"But I knew something happened. You just wouldn't tell me. You wouldn't let me in."

I frowned but nodded. "You're right. I moved here to start over. Somewhere people didn't look at me like maybe I was remembering this time because I drank milk with my pinky out or stirred my coffee with the back of my spoon. So, I bought myself a house and started over here. No expectations. I never planned on dating. At all. And then you came along."

"Well, I guess I should have listened."

"No. Please don't say that. These past few months have been amazing."

"So amazing that you ran into another man's arms when we were supposed to go away together." He pushed away from the desk and stood, pacing the space by the window.

"No, that's not it at all." Tears stung my eyes.

He blew out a breath.

"When I got my memories back, it was so overwhelming. Everything was so jumbled, and all I could think of was getting home to apologize for leaving everyone the way I did. I hardly gave them any notice. Two days. That's it. I had to apologize."

"I'm still missing the part where you end up with some guy, dressed like you're on a date."

*Yeah, that's the part you're really not going to like.*

I took a deep breath. "That guy was Jeremy, my ex."

Jack pushed his hands into his hair and shook his head. He didn't want to listen anymore. I needed to speed this up, or I'd lose him before he heard everything.

"I broke up with him when I moved here." I hesitated. "He was driving when we got into the accident."

This had his eyes back on me, curiosity roused.

"When everything came back to me, my mind was flooded with guilt over how heartlessly I broke up with him. He was my best friend. I had to see him, and then, after I saw him and got settled at my parents', I was so confused. I needed to know if any of what we had was still there before I came back. Before I continued the life I built here. I couldn't come back wondering. I couldn't do that to you . . . or him."

"So, it was a date?"

"Yes."

"Unbelievable. What about this is supposed to make me feel better?"

"Watching you walk away made everything clearer than ever. What Jeremy and I had doesn't even compare to how you make me feel."

"Did you kiss him?"

I winced. "Yes."

His face turned red, and I could see the hurt and anger bubbling under the surface. "Then there's nothing more to say. I have no interest in standing by while you're out kissing other people, just to see if you like them more."

"Please." Tears fell, running down my face. "Please don't end this. It was all a mistake. I should have told you. I was going to tell you everything while we were away, but then everything came back. It will never happen again . . ." I walked over and stood in front of him. Reaching out, I grabbed his hands. "I love you. Please."

His eyes flickered to mine. For just a second, I saw something in them—hope. Then, just as quick, it was gone, and he pulled away.

"It's over," he whispered.

"No. Please. Please don't do this." I reached out and grabbed his hand.

"Melanie." He pulled his hand away, and his face was all-business.

My lip quivered. My eyes fell to the floor. "I'll clear my things out."

He whipped around. "What?"

"The things at my desk. I'll take them with me."

"You're quitting?"

I paused, utterly perplexed. "You hired someone new . . . I assumed . . ."

"A temp."

"Oh. So, I still have a job?"

"I told you when we started seeing each other, it wouldn't affect our business relationship. I don't plan to go back on that. I expect you back here Monday."

I fought the urge to smile. "Thank you." I nodded once, though I'm not sure why, and left his office.

My body moved forward on autopilot; numbness settled its way throughout. I'd fallen in love, and now I was being cast aside, and it was all my fault. I didn't blame him. Not really. If the tables had been turned and I'd found out he kissed his ex the way I had, I'm not sure what I would do. Let alone to have such a big secret.

But at least I didn't have to find a new job. I never realized how grateful I'd be for his hermit-like nature at work. It sure would make it a lot easier to come back.

I moved past Sandra and Cindy and found myself sitting behind the wheel of my car, immobile. Tears clouded my eyes. Finally, I gave up and threw my keys back in my purse. It was best not to drive anyway.

I wanted to call Grace, but I just couldn't bear saying it out loud.

*He broke up with me.*

I stopped by the grocery store and got a tube of cookie dough and chocolate ice cream. It was cliché, but I didn't care—it would make me feel so much better. I only wished I would have thought to get spoons so I didn't have to wait. Wouldn't that have been a pretty sight, me eating ice cream from the carton, as I walked home with tears streaming down my face? Nobody needed to see that.

# Chapter
# FOURTEEN

**I SPENT THE** next few days in bed, indulging myself in the biggest sugar spree of the decade. Aside from getting my takeout lunch and dinner deliveries from the front door, I didn't budge. So far, I'd ignored all the calls from Grace and all but one of my dad's, in which I told him Jack wouldn't take me back after all and I didn't want to talk about it. That didn't stop him from calling though, repeatedly. Then there were the texts and a few calls from Jeremy. All left unanswered.

I didn't blame him. I never did say goodbye; however, by now I was sure the point had gotten across. I'd moved on.

It was the very last text that came in late that night, as I settled myself deeper into the pillows and pushed my top knot further up on my head, that had me sitting upright faster than I'd moved all week.

*Come open the door.*

I clicked off the TV that was blaring so loud, just so I didn't have to listen to the vibrating walls. The club down the way had really ramped it up for a Friday night. It only made me think of going there with Grace and where that night led, and it hurt all over again.

I tightened my top knot and glanced in the mirror. Yuck. I groaned. No time.

I hopped down the stairs two at a time and yanked the door open. There Jeremy stood, looking well put together and polished like he always did, though there were a few creases here and there. Instinctively, I pulled at my shirt.

*Like it would change how terrible I looked.*

"What are you doing here?" I asked.

"You didn't answer my calls or texts. I had to make sure you were okay."

He stepped inside and pulled me into his arms, shutting the door behind himself with his foot.

"You look a mess," he said into my hair. "And . . ." He sniffed.

"I know, I smell." I pulled away and tugged my hair down, then threw it back up, though I wasn't sure it made a difference.

"And this is your place?" He stepped into the living room.

"Yeah. How'd you know where I live?"

"Your dad."

I nodded.

I stared at the gray couch Jack helped me move in here. I could still hear him teasing me for not paying the extra fifty dollars for delivery. Of course, the tank of gas in the borrowed truck had cost me almost as much, and we'd still had to carry the thing ourselves. I never admitted he was right, but he was. Now it didn't matter anyway.

"It's really nice. Exactly what I'd pictured for you."

"Ha! You should have seen it when I moved in. I think the realtor thought I was crazy."

"Oh, yeah?"

I nodded.

"Look, I took such a late flight, I didn't have time for dinner. You mind if I order Chinese food or something?"

I stared at him. The thought that he'd be staying hadn't really occurred to me. "Oh, ah, of course. There are some menus on the fridge. I'm going to go take a shower . . . ah . . . I wasn't expecting anyone."

He grinned, scrunching his nose. "I figured."

I stuck my tongue out. I could hear him chuckle as I left the room.

When I returned, clean and fresh smelling, my living room and kitchen had been cleaned, and Jeremy had set the coffee table for two.

"You cleaned."

He shrugged. "Had a few free minutes."

"Thanks."

It wasn't until he finished eating and it was well into the early morning hours of the next day that I finally asked him the burning question.

"Why'd you come here?" It came out a lot harsher than I'd meant it, though it didn't seem to faze him.

"I told you. I was worried about you."

"So?"

He looked at the floor, then back at me. Hurt flickered in his eyes, but then it was gone. "I know I'm not the one. It wasn't one hundred percent clear to me until I showed up here tonight."

I froze, my breath held in my lungs.

He gave me a timid look. "I may have had some ideas about how tonight was going to go." He paused. "It's hard letting you go. I think you and I are more alike than I'd ever realized because this mess . . . it was me too . . . when you left."

"I'm sorry."

He shook his head. "Our history doesn't change our relationship; it only makes it stronger. We were friends first. Best friends. We always will be."

"You're the best." I leaned my head on his shoulder and yawned.

"That." He pointed at my open mouth. "Me too. I should get going. You don't have plans tomorrow?"

"That would be correct. I planned one more day of sulking."

He chuckled. "Good. You have to show me around your new town."

"Where are you staying?"

He made a face. "The first hotel I can find."

"What?!"

"Truth be told, this was a bit spontaneous."

"Well, forget it. You can stay here if you don't mind the couch. I do have an air mattress, but I think the couch is a lot more comfortable."

"Are you sure? It's not a big deal to find somewhere."

"Of course. I'm not going to send you out at this hour, trying to find a place to stay, when I have a perfectly good couch right here."

He smiled. "Thanks. I'll go get my things."

"I'm going to head up to bed. Okay?"

"Goodnight."

"Night." I turned back halfway up the stairs, just before he stepped outside. "Jeremy?"

"Yeah."

"I'm really glad you came."

"Me too."

The next morning, I woke when the smell of coffee and bacon drifted up to me. Curiosity pulled me out of bed. I didn't even own a coffee pot, and I was sure there wasn't a single package of bacon in the house.

Jeremy sat on the couch with a newspaper in his hands, sipping coffee from a paper cup. He'd gone down to the coffeehouse, somewhere I'd been avoiding like the plague despite the craving deep in my gut. A second cup and paper bag sat on the coffee table.

I watched him for a moment, taking in the sight. It felt so good having him here, like a little piece of home had made its way in.

"Hey. Morning."

"Morning," I grumbled, my voice garbled from sleep.

"I got you some coffee and breakfast. I hope you still like what you used to get."

I sipped the coffee, the vanilla-flavored warmth slid down my throat as he pulled out the contents of the bag. "You remembered."

"Of course. They thought I was strange for wanting syrup for your bacon, egg, and cheese sandwich though."

I giggled. "They're all just missing out."

He shook his head, making a face. "I don't know about that."

He put down the paper and glanced at the corner where I'd left the sewing machine set up. "You're sewing again?"

I nodded. "That night I found my sketchbook, I drew a new dress and sewed it. Stayed up all night." I laughed.

"It always gave you so much joy to finish something. I remember how excited you'd be when you'd call to tell me you'd finished."

I thought of the thrill I'd felt just over a week ago. "Still does. I'd actually decided that's what I was going to do. And now. . ." I trailed off, unsure of what I wanted now.

After we finished eating, I grabbed all the garbage and headed into the kitchen to toss it. Jeremy followed behind.

"I think you should. You've always been really talented at creating beautiful things."

I smiled. "What do you want to do today?"

"You're the local. You tell me."

I thought for a second and smiled. "Actually, I was planning to go for a hike. Figured it'd be a good way to clear my head before I go back to work on Monday. There's this trail that's practically in my back yard. It's really pretty."

"I'm in."

"You have shoes, right?" I glanced at his flip flop-clad feet.

"Of course."

Two hours later, we made it to my favorite place on the trail, a small stream. The calm waters trickling through the rocks relaxed me. I sat on the big rock I always tended to gravitate towards.

Jeremy came up behind me and rested his hands on my shoulders. For a while, we just stood there and watched the water, listening to it run through the rocks.

"What's on your mind?"

"Facing Jack on Monday at work."

"At work?"

"Jack's my boss." I looked into his eyes, knowing he wouldn't like that. Nobody did, though he showed no emotion.

"That's going to be rough."

"I know, I know. That's why you don't date your boss. Trust me, I never would have if I'd known he was my boss before I let my thoughts go there."

"No judgment." He held up his hands.

"Right."

"Are you okay?"

I sighed. "I will be."

He pressed his fingers into the knots in my shoulders, rubbing in circles. "Is there anything I can do?"

"You're already doing more than I realized I needed."

Jeremy let me have a few more minutes locked away in my thoughts before he spoke again. "Come on, let's go explore." He pulled me to my feet.

I followed him around for a while before we stumbled upon the tiniest of waterfalls. Maybe it couldn't even be considered a waterfall, since it only fell about ten inches.

"It looks like there's a hole behind it." Jeremy squatted down, squinting against the glare of sunlight cast off the water.

"Is there?" I leaned down behind him, trying to see. "Reach in, see how big."

"No! You don't know what's in there."

"Come on. Don't be a sissy. You know you want to know what's back there just as bad as I do."

He glared at me before he knelt and looked at the waterfall again. His hand disappeared inside, the water cascading around his wrist. I held my breath.

"Oh my gosh. What do you feel?"

He made a face and pulled his hand out. "Slimy stone."

"Anything back there?"

He shook his head and wiped his hand on his shorts. "Nope, but it'd be a good hiding place. It's a little bit bigger than my hand."

"How cool. I might have to come back and hide something in there."

"Ha! I'd love to see you stick your hand in there!"

My hands went to my hips. "Rude!"

We made the trek back a few hours later, after exploring the area more than I'd been adventurous enough to do.

"I could really go for a big pepperoni pizza right now. I'm starving."

"Mmm," he groaned, "you're making my stomach grumble. Those sandwiches we packed didn't stay with me for very long."

Jeremy pushed the door closed behind him as I pulled out all the menus.

"Mind if I take a quick shower?" he asked.

"Go ahead. I'm going to take one too, but I'll order the pizza first. Want anything else?"

"Nope, just pizza."

Thirty minutes later, I was toweling off my hair when the doorbell rang. "That's probably the pizza, will you grab it? I'll be right down!" I yelled.

"Okay," Jeremy called up the stairs.

Seconds later, loud voices penetrated my quiet house.

"What are you doing here?" someone shouted.

"Melanie?" Jeremy's worried voice drifted up to me.

In seconds, I was at the foot of the stairs. Jeremy had backed away from the door, and Jack stood just inside the door, bright red in the face. He was fuming.

"Jack."

"What the hell is this, Melanie?" he demanded. "It's only been a few days, and you've already moved on? I should have known."

"Jeremy came to make sure I was okay."

"I can't believe I came here, thinking I'd been a jerk, ready to apologize for ending things the way I did. And you are here . . . with him."

"This isn't what you think."

"Really? Because it looks like you're with your ex-boyfriend, the same one you went on a date with *while* we were still together, on the very weekend we were supposed to go away together."

"We're just friends."

"Right. Friends who look like they've both just showered. Perfect."

"Separately. We just got back from a hike."

He put up his hand to stop me. "Save it."

"Jack."

He turned and marched down the steps.

I spun to face Jeremy.

He mouthed, "Go."

It was all I needed, and I took off running. This was it. My last chance to go after him like I hadn't before. After this moment, there was no going back. I'd never be able to work for him again after this, if I couldn't get him to change his mind.

"Jack," I shouted. "Wait."

He froze with his back to me.

"I love you. Please. Can we talk?"

"What is there to talk about? It looks to me like you've already moved on."

"I haven't. I've spent the last few days in bed, ignoring everyone. I've been so . . . heartbroken. Jeremy was worried, so he flew out here to check on me. He got me out of bed, but as a friend. There's nothing between us anymore, he knows that. And if you'd ask him, he would tell you."

He whirled around to face me. "How am I supposed to believe you? You've been lying to me for months."

"I haven't. I told you something bad happened, and I didn't want to talk about it. But I should have. I should have told you everything right from the start. I know that. I'll tell you anything you want to know. No more secrets, I swear. From now on, nothing but honesty." I reached for his arm.

His eyes closed, but he didn't shake it off, so I stepped closer.

"Melanie," Jeremy said from behind me. I glanced over my shoulder. His bags were already at his feet. "I should go."

"Yes, you *really* should." Jack ground his teeth together.

"Jack." I placed my hand on his arm. He threw it up, knocking my hand off. I sighed and looked over at Jeremy. "I thought you weren't leaving until tomorrow."

"It's time." Jeremy eyed Jack.

I nodded, knowing what he meant. He was stepping out of the situation to let us figure things out. "Thanks for coming. I owe you."

"It's what we do for friends. Take care of yourself. Okay?" He loaded his bags into the trunk of his rental car but stopped and looked at Jack. "She's pretty special, not someone who betrays on purpose. Take care of her, okay? Better than I did." He nodded to Jack and got in the car.

The last part of his statement hit me right in the gut. The guilt he still felt over the accident, which ultimately had pulled me away from him.

It appeared as though Jeremy's words were what gave Jack the last nudge he needed. His eyes were on me when my attention flickered back to him, intense and searching.

"There's really nothing between the two of you?"

I shook my head. "I swear."

The next second, he kissed me. I gripped onto him, and I never wanted to let go. I'd been craving his touch all week, ever since I'd walked out of his office, crushed. And now I had it, and it was better than it ever had been before.

"Ahem, I have a pizza delivery," a timid voice said from behind Jack.

I laughed against Jack's lips. "You hungry?"

"Always."

I took the pizza, letting the guy get back to work. Jack turned to walk inside when a thought struck me.

"Ah, one more thing . . . you know, with the 'no secrets' thing . . ."

He turned slowly, his face serious.

"I never told you, but I feel like I should." I pressed my finger to my lip. "I have a trust."

Relief flooded his features. He pulled me into his arms, tossing the pizza box onto the hood of his car. "You didn't want to tell me you had money?"

"I guess we both didn't want anyone to distinguish us because of it."

He laughed. "Now I know we're perfect for each other."

***

### Three weeks later . . .

"Are you ready yet?" Jack called up the stairs.

I pushed my suitcase to the edge of the stairs. "Yes."

"Finally!" Then he looked at the size of my bag. "Really?"

"What?"

"You could fit inside of that bag."

"So?"

"It's only going to be a couple days." He came up the stairs to retrieve it.

"But it's *Christmas*."

He grinned down at me. "It's going to be the best Christmas." He kissed my forehead. "Even if I break my back carrying this bag around."

"Ha. Ha." I made a face at him.

An hour later, Jack pulled the car into a drive, which I could tell hadn't been driven on since it snowed last. Not a single tire tracked through its whiteness. The trees, however, were heaping with snow, allowing a thin powder to fall between their branches. We curved around through the large pines before a huge cabin appeared before us. The enormity of it was startling.

"How many bedrooms does this place have?"

Jack chuckled. "Six."

Nothing like the average persona he tried to keep up back home.

He opened the door, and the cold air whipped me in the face. "Brrr." I shivered.

"Well, I'd be willing to bet Rose has a fire going inside."

I clutched my purse to my chest, absorbing the last of its warmth, as he got my bag out of the back. I bounced up and down, trying to keep my legs warm. "I hope so. It's sooo cold!"

"Come on."

The moment we stepped through the double front doors, the cold was long forgotten as the warmth from inside welcomed and the beauty from within captivated me.

"Pretty amazing, right?"

"*Yes.*" I spun around, looking at the entryway from all angles.

"My mom spent a fortune trying to get it just right."

"I bet."

He led me upstairs and showed me to a room to the right. "This will be your room. Unless . . . ." He paused and stepped from the room to the room across the hall, which was quite a bit larger. A fire was already warming the room. "You'd like to stay in the same room. I'm fine either way, but I didn't want to be presumptuous."

He acted like he was going to wait for my answer, then quickly turned around. "I'm going to find Rose and let you make that decision."

I muffled my giggles behind my hand. I'd never seen him nervous before. What he didn't realize was, I never pictured us staying in separate rooms.

I heaved my bag onto its wheels and rolled it into our room. *Our* room. I liked the sound of that.

I found Jack, after at least ten minutes of searching, in the kitchen with an older woman. She had graying short hair and was plump around the middle. They were hunched over the stove, talking in hushed tones, while she stirred something in a pot.

"Mmmm, what's that I smell? I can almost taste it."

Both Jack and the woman jumped at the sound of my voice.

"Fresh apple cider. Would you care for some?" the woman asked.

"Yes, please."

"Rose, I'd like you to meet my girlfriend, Melanie."

"It's good to meet you." She held out a steaming mug.

"You too. Thank you."

She smiled at the two of us like a grandmother would, with love and fondness.

"Come on," he said.

He led me out of the kitchen. I couldn't be sure, but I thought I saw him turn back to her and wink.

"Where are we going?" I asked.

"Snowmobiling."

"What? It's freezing out there!"

"Trust me, you're going to love it!"

I stopped just short of the door leading to the garage, breathing in the warm spice from my mug, and took one last gulp, allowing it to glide down and warm me from the inside before I stepped out into the garage. I braced for the cold. It didn't come.

"It's warm in here."

"The garage is heated."

"What? That's crazy."

"Not after you've been in the cold for an hour and need the warmth."

I shook my head. "No, that's still crazy. You just go in the house."

He chuckled. "Here."

He handed me a pair of snow coveralls with full arms and full legs. I stepped into it, and he stepped into a pair that was similar.

"Whose are these?" I asked.

"My mom's."

Phew. I was glad they weren't Bianca's. Somehow, I didn't feel comfortable wearing anything of hers. I wasn't sure how much she actually approved of me, even though she'd been perfectly nice ever since the barbecue.

He climbed onto the seat of one of the three snowmobiles and patted behind him for me to get on. "Unless you'd prefer to drive yourself?"

"Oh no, I think my hands would be frozen." I hurried and climbed on the back of his.

He took me all over the woods without any particular goal in mind. I could tell this was where he felt the most at home, the woods. And he was right, I was having a lot of fun. Who'd have thought?

He sped up as he approached a small mound of snow, launching us into the air just a little. I squealed, reaching around his waist, giving him a squeeze. He slammed on the brakes and turned around.

Before I knew what he was doing, his mouth was on mine. The warmth of his tongue sent sensations through my lips I'd never experienced. They tingled like your whole body would when immersed in a hot tub after being in the cold, and it was heavenly. He pulled away too quickly, and I tugged him back. His mouth lifted at the corners against mine. When I pulled back, I rested my forehead on his.

I sighed, content.

"Had to make sure your nose was staying warm," he said.

"Oh, yeah?"

"What did you find?"

"I think it's in need of a little warming up."

"I concur. What do you suggest?"

He pressed his nose against mine and rubbed back and forth. "Eskimo kisses."

I giggled. He planted another kiss at the tip of my nose, spun around, and took off again, zipping over another mound.

It wasn't until the sun dipped out of view that the cold really set in and the coveralls stopped doing their job. I shivered as he hurried to get us back to the house.

He pulled straight into the garage and shut the door. It was then I realized how right he was. A heated garage was amazing after coming in from snowmobiling.

Jack immediately started stripping out of the coveralls. "The faster you get out of them, the faster you'll warm up. It's a fact."

I grinned at him. "Sure it is."

He waited at the door and held it open for me to go in before him. The lights had been dimmed in the entire house. Red and white rose petals littered the floor.

Jack slipped his hand into mine. I looked up into his green eyes.

"Go on." He gestured for me to follow the path the roses created.

White candles were lit on every table, in all different shapes and sizes.

"What is all this?" I smiled back at Jack.

We turned the last corner towards the dining room, where the table was set for two. Silver cloches covered two plates, and two tall candles rose up in the center.

Jack came up beside me and lifted the cover on the closest plate, and my mouth fell open. I'd never before gawked at a plate with such scrutiny. My mouth fell open.

Scrolled in chocolate were the words, "Will you marry me?"

Jack dropped to his knee and flipped open a tiny box. "I know it hasn't been very long, and things got a little rocky, but I've never felt the way I feel when I'm with you, ever. I know, deep within my heart, this is my destiny. *Our* destiny. I hope with every part of me you'll say yes and make me the happiest I've ever been in my life. Marry me."

I bit my lip as the corners of my mouth lifted. "Yes."

"Yes?"

I nodded, laughing. "Yes."

He slipped the ring on my finger and pressed his lips to mine with a hunger he often had. That hunger pulled me in and swooped me off my feet, making me feel like I was floating. And now I'd feel that way for the rest of my life.

"I love you," he whispered into my hair.

"I love you too."

"She said *yes!*" Jack yelled, turning away from me.

I scrunched my face, squeezing him around the neck. "Nobody can hear you, crazy. We're alone, remember?" I giggled.

Footsteps and loud whoops came flooding into the room. I pulled away just as Jack's family came bursting in, full of excitement. Much to my surprise, my mom and dad rounded the corner behind them.

"Mom? Dad?" Tears stung in my eyes.

My worlds were finally colliding in a way I never dreamed they could. My home had nothing to do with geography and everything to do with the people I called family, and ones who soon would be.

Sometimes things happen, unexpected and out of the blue. Things you never thought could, or would, happen. Things you would never want to prevent. The ones you dream of, hope for, sure they'll never come true.

Sometimes those things are put in your lap and all you have to do is take them. Those are the moments that every wager up until that point has been leading up to. Every choice.

This was that moment. The point in my life I knew, no matter how much I'd struggled with every choice I'd made, I knew they were all the exact right ones because they'd led me to a happiness I could never have dreamed possible.

As our families descended upon us, hugging and grabbing my hand to steal their first looks at the ring, I looked up at Jack, smiling, with his eyes alight. This man would be mine forever, and nothing excited me more.

# MORE

Thank you for checking out Wagering Home. I truly hope you enjoyed it.

I'd love to hear what you thought, please consider leaving a review on Amazon, Goodreads, and/or the retailer of your choice to help other readers find this book.

More from C. M. Boers:
**Obscured**
**Divulge**
**Derailed**
**Retreat**

Like to stay in touch with me? Find out about upcoming releases, giveaways, and events at **www.cmboers.com**.

**Facebook**
**Instagram**